P9-DZP-209

Dear America

The Diary of Pringle Rose

DOWN THE RABBIT HOLE

Susan Campbell Bartoletti

SCHOLASTIC INC. • NEW YORK

In memory of Sal Angello
(1947–2010),
an exceptional person in every sense of the word

Library of Congress Cataloging-in-Publication Data

Bartoletti, Susan Campbell.
Down the rabbit hole : the diary of Pringle Rose / Susan Campbell Bartoletti.
– 1st ed.
p. cm. – (Dear America)
Summary: It is 1871 in Scranton, Pennsylvania, and fourteen-year-old Pringle
Rose, still grieving from the death of her parents, takes her brother, Gideon,
who has Down syndrome, and escapes from her uncle and aunt, on a train to
Chicago – but disaster seems to follow her there.
ISBN 978-0-545-29701-1
1. Great Fire, Chicago, Ill., 1871–Juvenile fiction. 2. Orphans–Juvenile fiction.
3. Down syndrome–Juvenile fiction. 4. Children with mental disabilities–
Juvenile fiction. 5. Diaries–Juvenile fiction. 6. Chicago (Ill.)–History–19th
century–Juvenile fiction. 7. Scranton (Pa.)–History–19th century–Juvenile
fiction. 8. Diary fiction. [1. Great Fire, Chicago, Ill., 1871–Fiction. 2. Orphans–
Fiction. 3. Runaways–Fiction. 4. Down syndrome–Fiction. 5. People with
mental disabilities–Fiction. 6. Diaries–Fiction. 7. Chicago (Ill.)–History–19th
century–Fiction. 8. Scranton (Pa.)–History–19th century–Fiction.] I. Title.
II. Series: Dear America.
PZ7.B2844Do 2013
813.54–dc23
2012023693

10 9 8 7 6 5 4 3 2 1 13 14 15 16 17

The text type was set in ITC Legacy Serif.
The display type was set in Runic MT.
Book design by Kevin Callahan
Photo research by Amla Sanghvi

Printed in the U.S.A. 23
First edition, March 2013

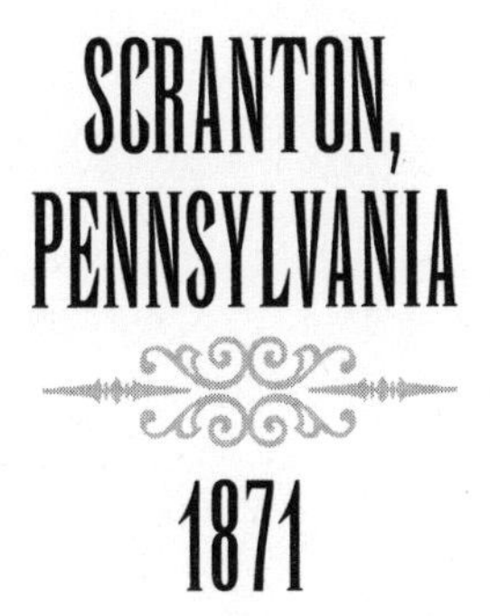
SCRANTON,
PENNSYLVANIA
1871

MONDAY, SEPTEMBER 4, 1871
9:30 A.M.

At last my hands have stopped shaking and I can write. I must write everything down, as best I can.

If anything happens to me, I entreat the finder of this diary to send these pages to Miss Mary Catherine Fisher at Merrywood School for Girls in Philadelphia.

Merricat is my favorite friend and she wants to be an authoress. In these pages she will find a good, sad story to tell. If the worst comes to me, I authorize Merricat to release my story to the world.

A GOOD, SAD STORY

At 9:00 A.M. sharp this morning, the train whistled and snorted a great puff of smoke. Gideon clapped his hands over his ears and grinned at me. He loves whistles and bells.

I forced a smile. I didn't tell Gideon that my stomach was twisting into one very hard knot. As the great wheels turned beneath us, a sour taste rose in my mouth. I worried that I might need a polite place to vomit.

To settle my stomach, I concentrated on our journey. With each *chuff* of the mighty Lackawanna's engine, Scranton slid farther into the distance and the hard knot loosened. Soon the train's steady rhythm comforted me. I told myself that the train was galloping Gideon and me toward safety and a new life.

I squeezed Gideon's hand and turned my head so that he wouldn't see the hot, salty tears streaming down my face.

Dear, sweet Gideon! He always senses when something is wrong, and because he's a gentleman, he tries to fix it. He took out his white handkerchief and offered it to me.

I dabbed my eyes and cheeks and chin. "It's nothing but a cinder," I told him. "All better now, see?"

He folded the handkerchief four times into a neat square and tucked it into his shirt pocket.

From his vest pocket, Gideon took out his gold pocket watch, a gift from Father when Gideon learned to tell time. He pressed the clasp, springing open the lid.

I settled back against the car's seat and let my thoughts fly forward. "We'll reach Chicago Wednesday morning," I told him.

Gideon moved his fingers and held up three.

"That's right," I told him. "Three days. You count very well."

Gideon leaned against me. He smelled like spice and bergamot and orange blossoms. "Are you wearing Father's cologne?" I asked him.

He nodded.

I AM A THIEF

Last night, when the last sliver of gaslight dimmed beneath each bedroom door, I rose from bed.

There's an art to walking soundlessly. It's something Merricat and I learned to do exceedingly well on our night escapes from the dormitory. To move soundlessly, you shuffle. You distribute your weight evenly in small flat steps. You move lightly but with great purpose.

With great purpose, I moved down the dark hallway and downstairs. Neither a bump nor stir nor rustle did anyone hear.

I groped my way to Father's library and turned the brass doorknob. The door whispered against the thick rug.

Moonlight spilled through Father's office window. The dark shapes shifted into Father's high-backed chair, his green lamp, and his coat rack. On his rows of books, the gilt lettering glinted.

A hunched form rose from Father's chair, its eyes glowing, its tail flagpole straight. "*Me-owrch,*" said Mozie.

He leaped to the floor with a soft thump and rubbed against my legs. "Shhh," I said, picking him up. "You're not supposed to be here. You've been banished, remember? You'll lose all nine lives if you get caught."

With my lap full of cat, I tugged open the middle desk drawer, groped for the false divider, and lifted it out. I patted inside the hidden compartment until I found the drawstring sack of gold and silver coins.

My heart pounded so hard against my chest, I felt it in my ears. There were fifty dollars in all.

Heavy! I swaddled the coins in my nightdress. Then I carried Mozie and the coins upstairs.

On my bed, Mozie kneaded me with his paws, purring. I lay there, staring at the full moon over the trees.

Did I sleep? I must have, for the next thing I heard was the tread of feet passing my bedroom, so heavy they sounded as if they carried the weight of the world.

Nervous! I could hardly breathe! I retraced my steps. Did I remember to close Father's office? Yes.

Return the hidden panel? Yes.

Close the desk drawer? Yes.

Had I left anything out of place? No.

Had anyone heard me? Seen me? Suspected me?

I prayed not.

I counted the morning sounds, ticking each off. Muffled voices. The slam of the back door. The jingle of a horse in its traces. The clatter of a carriage down the alley.

Next, a serving tray rattled up the back stairway. Two sharp raps on a bedroom door. Another door opened and closed. Then footsteps back to the kitchen.

I slipped from bed and pulled a plain blue dress over my head, and then yanked a black dress over the blue. I carried Mozie across the hall into Gideon's room and plunked the cat on top of him.

"Get dressed," I told him.

Gideon's eyes popped open. He shook his head no and pulled the covers to his chin. He remembered he was being punished.

"We're going on an adventure," I said. "Just like Alice. We mustn't be late."

Excitement flooded his face. He rolled out of bed and dressed quickly.

I packed our carpetbags: two changes of clothing and other necessities, Mother's scarlet cloak and Bible, my worn copy of *Alice's Adventures in Wonderland*, and the letter from Mother's favorite friend, Beatrice Ringwald.

Gideon and I bade good morning to our cook, Mrs. Robson, who trilled back, "Good morrrning" in her Scottish burr.

We ate hotcakes and sausages. We stacked our dishes by the sink. I set a saucer of milk on the kitchen floor for Mozie.

Mozie purred as he lapped up the milk. As soon as Mrs. Robson went outside to tend her kitchen garden, I wrapped a chunk of bread, a wedge of cheese, four sausages, four apples, and the best paring knife in a plain white cloth.

Our housekeeper, Mrs. Goodwin, caught me. She opened the cloth. "A picnic, eh?"

My heart raced.

"That lunch will never do you." She added six hard-boiled eggs, six boiled potatoes in their jackets, two cucumbers, and the last of the sausages, and wrapped everything back up. "God be with you," she said.

Did Mrs. Goodwin know? Did I hear a sniffle? I kissed her cheek—it was wet—and thanked her for the picnic.

We left no note.

We let ourselves out the front door.

It was a perfectly lovely morning, the cicadas

already humming, the birds calling to one another, squirrels arguing. In plain sight, we strolled down Olive Street.

Suddenly, wheels clattered around the corner. Hooves struck the brick street. My heart pounded against my ribs. I sucked in my breath. Had we been found out? Should we run?

The driver shouted, "Hallo, Miss Pringle! Hallo, Master Gideon! Where are you off to this fine morning? Would you like a lift?"

It was Mr. York, our huckster. "No, thank you!" I shouted back, and waved him on. The horse snorted and swished her tail. The cart rattled by, loaded with cabbages, turnips, potatoes, and apples. I could breathe again.

THE STOWAWAY

We passed the streets named after our presidents and made our way downhill to Wyoming Avenue. Busy! Carriages raced up and down the street. Men wearing frock coats and tall hats and watches on gold chains rushed importantly from one building to another. Here and there, women in ruffled walking dresses wore hats perched jauntily at an angle and carried bright parasols.

I clutched Gideon's hand, so we wouldn't get separated. We followed Lackawanna Avenue to the train station. He stood outside the washroom. I slipped inside and yanked off my black mourning weeds, exposing the plain blue dress underneath.

In the looking glass, a strange girl stared back at me. Her black hair was loose and wild. She had a delicate face with intense green eyes and a stubborn chin. She was a thief, absconding with a sack of gold and silver coins stolen from her father's desk and food stolen from the family kitchen and a brother stolen from his bed.

I repinned my hair. I didn't want to think about the girl in the looking glass.

Outside, I stuffed the black dress in a barrel. I grabbed Gideon's hand and led him to the ticket counter, where I purchased the tickets. The ticket agent yawned and barely glanced at us as he slid the tickets across the counter.

We found our car and I let Gideon sit by the

window. Before long, the train hissed and snorted its great breath. The conductor called out, "All aboard!"

At the very last moment, a harried-looking woman in a pink dress with two chattering children and a baby in tow climbed aboard and filled the seat behind us.

As the train pulled away from the station, Gideon's carpetbag swelled and growled.

I gasped. "You didn't!" I unsnapped his carpetbag, and oh, my paws and whiskers! A white paw shot out and swiped at the air.

Gideon grinned.

"Oh, you! What are we going to do with Mozie?" I pretended to be annoyed, but secretly I was happy that Mozie was safe with us, because he didn't have many lives left. Besides, Alice's cat, Dinah, never did get to Wonderland, did she?

Now Mozie sleeps in the carpetbag at our feet and the train puffs north like a great racehorse through the prettiest oaks and maples and pines. The little girl behind me keeps kicking my seat. She makes my teeth rattle.

Ten thirty A.M. We've been underway for over an hour. Gideon stares out the window as if he hopes train robbers will burst out. A few minutes ago, he nudged me and pointed to a large buck with a full rack of antlers standing at the fringe of the woods.

Behind us, a red-haired boy with a freckled face stuck his right arm straight out and pointed his fingers like a rifle at the buck. "Pow," he said. Then he wheeled his arm around and pointed his finger at Gideon. "Powpowpow!"

The boy ducked. He poked his head over the seat. "Got you."

"Adam," said his mother. "You mustn't pester."

Adam's mother looks tired, no doubt from minding three children. Beside her sits a small girl with large brown eyes and a cupid face and feet that use my seat for a drum. On her lap, the mother holds a chubby baby girl who doesn't talk but points and says, "Ah ah ah."

I want Gideon to stick up for himself. I lifted his arm and folded down his thumb and three fingers and aimed his pointy finger back at the boy. "Pow," I whispered. "Say it. Pow."

Gideon wiggled free. But his face glowed with keen interest and wistfulness. He longs to play. He longs for a true friend.

A favorite friend is worth waiting for. I never had one until I found Merricat, or as Merricat says, she found me. Someday, Gideon will find a true friend. It's just a matter of time. I know it. Just as I know a new life awaits us in Chicago.

THE NIGHTMARE

It's hard to write with a dip pen on a train, but I must write everything down. I'll begin at the beginning and go on from there, just as the King of Hearts tells Alice in Wonderland.

Our nightmare began last April. It was just before afternoon vespers, and Miss Westcott handed me two letters, one from Mother and one from Father.

How glad I felt to see Father's strong, angular hand and Mother's crisp, curling strokes. I missed my parents more than words can say.

Miss Westcott handed Merricat a thick envelope from her mother.

"Godey's Lady's Book," whispered Merricat, and we grinned.

I stuck the letters in my uniform pocket. Later, Merricat and I would lie across her bed and pore over *Godey's Lady's Book*, studying the latest fashions and styles, and longing for them. We would read our letters aloud, as we always did, just as we shared our diaries.

That day – the 13th of April – is the last time I remember feeling truly happy and carefree. Merricat and I linked arms, and since Miss Westcott wasn't looking, we skipped arm in arm to chapel. We didn't give one whit what the other girls thought.

We slid into our pew. It was raining, and the rain sounded like pebbles against the chapel roof and windows. I shivered and drew my shawl closer around me.

Two candles burned brightly on the altar. As the Reverend Porter droned on, I fingered the embossed letters on Mother's envelope. A breeze brushed against the nape of my neck, turning my skin to gooseflesh. On the altar table, the candles flamed brighter, and the faintest, most delicate scent of jasmine and violet floated in the air. It was Mother's exact perfume, one designed especially for her.

I sniffed, drawing it in, and turned my head. I was shocked to see Mother, her scarlet cloak draped around her shoulders. She smiled lovingly and held out her arms.

"Mother!" I said, popping to my feet. I threw my arms around her.

The Reverend Porter halted mid-sentence. Over half-glasses that reflected orange and yellow and white candlelight, he scolded me with his eyes.

Someone snickered.

Mother disappeared. I had thrown my arms around empty air.

"Miss Rose," said Miss Westcott. "That's enough of your antics. Sit down."

A heavy, dark feeling pulled me down into the pew.

All that day I carried that dark weight. I tried to lose myself in the parsing of sentences and the declension of Latin nouns and Trigonometry and Botany and French and German classes. Not my classmates' chirping nor Merricat's bright gossip nor *Godey's Lady's Book* could lift the heavy cloud.

That night, I comforted myself with the letters from Mother and Father. Father wrote about the coal miners' strike, now entering its fifth month. Father called the Workmen's Benevolent Society "evil" and said that the labor group was hurting the miners. He said it was turning them into criminals who burned breakers and destroyed the personal property of colliery operators. He vowed never to capitulate to the workers' demands for higher wages.

Mother asked about my studies. She hoped I was meeting the right people. She reminded me that whom one meets is important in shaping a girl's future. Mother often included her favorite Bible quotes and wrote little instructions in her letters, asking if I was reading my Bible and reminding me to pray.

The answer was yes and yes. I was reading my Bible and I was praying. That night, while my classmates slumbered around me, I lifted the door latch and escaped into the hallway. As the moonlight spilled through the window, I knelt and clasped my hands together and closed my eyes and prayed as Jabez had prayed in 1 Chronicles 4:10: I prayed for God to bless me and to enlarge my coast and to guide me with His hand and to keep evil from me.

There was so much I wanted. I wanted a larger life. I wanted to travel and to study and to do all sorts of things. Was it wrong? Was it selfish and greedy for a girl to want more than she has?

When I opened my eyes, the hallway brightened for a second. In that glowing second I believed that my prayer was answered, too. Then a cloud passed over the moon, darkening the window.

The next morning, Miss Westcott came to the doorway of our German class. "Come," she said, beckoning me with her finger.

Merricat reached across the aisle, her eyes wide

and worrying. She squeezed my trembling hand and mouthed, "What did you do?"

I mouthed back, "I don't know."

I followed Miss Westcott's swishing crinoline skirts. Oh, the thoughts that tumbled through my head! The last girl summoned to Miss Westcott's office was dismissed for breaking the school's honor code.

Did Miss Westcott know I had climbed the bluff overlooking the chapel?

That Merricat and I had hung unladylike from the tree outside the dormitory? Our skirts parasol-like over our faces? Our pantaloons showing?

That we stayed up past curfew, gossiping about our classmates and poring over *Godey's Lady's Book* by the light of a candle stub?

That we had perfected the art of walking soundlessly through the dormitory corridors?

Alas, how I wish it were one – or all! – of these things, for there, standing in Miss Westcott's office, was my father's only brother, Edward. The two rarely spoke and never agreed on anything.

I didn't need to read my uncle's face with my

eyes. I read his face with my insides. Something was terribly, dreadfully wrong.

THE THINGS I REMEMBER

I remember the rain pelted Miss Westcott's window.

I remember the rivulets of water streamed down the glass, making the trees, the outbuildings, the grass appear wavy.

I remember Uncle Edward's wet shoes squeaked against the wooden floor as he shifted his weight.

I remember his trousers were soaked from the knees down.

I remember he reeked of Hoyt's Cologne, a scent that Mother described as an attempt at a garden or a harvest or pickling. (A gentleman should be seen and not smelled.)

I remember his voice crackled like static air before a storm. "Pringle, I have terrible news."

Yet I plunged ahead, unafraid. I was Alice, chasing the White Rabbit. "It's Gideon," I said.

I have been prepared to lose my brother ever since he was a baby. Doctors say children like Gideon don't live to adulthood.

That's why my first thought was Gideon.

That's why my second thought was, *Please, let it be Gideon.*

Uncle Edward's words crashed like thunder. "It's not Gideon. I'm so sorry, Pringle. It's your parents."

My heart! I gripped the back of an upholstered chair to steady myself. "Are they sick?"

I knew the answer from his stricken look.

He circled my shoulders clumsily with his arm and steered me toward the divan. "There's no delicate way to put this. Come. Sit."

I rooted my feet to the carpet. "Then don't put it delicately."

"My dear niece," said Uncle Edward, taking my hand. "There's been a terrible accident. A carriage accident. Your mother and father are dead."

Dead! The word surged through me like lightning. I yanked my hand from my uncle's lest his hand singe mine.

"When?"

"Yesterday. I came as quickly as I could."

"Impossible!" I laughed as I reached in my

uniform pocket for my parents' letters. The joke was on my uncle. "How can they be dead? See? Here are their letters. They arrived yesterday." I knew the illogic even as I said it. My laugh sounded somewhere outside myself.

"I'm so sorry for your loss, my dear child," said Miss Westcott, drawing near.

How can I explain the feeling? Imagine your mind closing. The blood draining from your head and neck. Your mouth opens, but your throat closes around your words. Your arms, your legs, they go numb.

I was Alice, tumbling headlong down a deep, dark rabbit hole. The walls in Miss Westcott's office with their portraits of dour-faced headmistresses, the leather-bound books with gilt lettering, the tall pendulum clock, the gold-rimmed teacup and saucer, all these things spiraled so slowly it felt as though I could have reached out and sipped a cup of tea, just as Alice did.

Words wound about me, too. Words like *home* and *funeral* and *arrangements* sounded near and then from someplace deep and far away.

"Gideon?" I managed to squeak out.

"A few scrapes and bruises."

And this was my third thought, which I said out loud: "Why isn't it Gideon? God took the wrong ones!"

"Priscilla Rose! You don't mean that," said Miss Westcott.

Why do adults tell you what you mean and don't mean? I did mean every word, and I would have said so, except the floor rushed at me with a roar and swallowed me. The next thing I knew, my nostrils felt as though they had exploded. I was lying on the divan, sputtering and snorting and gasping for air.

Miss Westcott capped the smelling salts. "Priscilla, God has a plan. You must believe that."

I struggled to sit up, and when I did, I looked at my uncle, heaved, and threw up in Miss Westcott's lap.

BINGHAMTON, NEW YORK
NOON

Not long after the train crossed the wide Susquehanna River, a blue-uniformed conductor moved through our car, shouting, "Bing-hamton!" Gideon loves uniforms and anybody who wears a uniform. He followed the conductor with admiring eyes.

We gathered our belongings and piled off the train and found our way to the Erie station next door. Behind us, the Lackawanna train pulled away with a great snort and hiss and cloud of black smoke. We hadn't a very long wait, just enough time to gobble our lunch and stretch our legs. The Erie train was scheduled for 1:20.

I opened the carpetbag, and Mozie leaped out, a tumble of legs and swishing tail and elongated meow. He stretched, groomed himself, and then slinked off to do his business. Mozie is a tame and proper cat.

Near us, Adam's mother has her hands full. The bigger little girl is named Lucy, and she is four years old. She is kicking up pebbles and dirt with her shoes, and whatever she does, her baby sister, Sallie, does, too. Her mother has scolded Lucy and told her "no" three times, which is two more chances than my mother would have given me.

1:10 P.M.

Guess who helped that mother? I did. With a sharp rock, I scratched out a hopscotch court in the dirt, and soon Lucy, Adam, and Gideon were taking turns. Gideon is good at sharing and taking turns, but not hopping. He hops with both feet, barely clearing the ground. In his mind's eye, he hops like a frog.

The hopscotch game gave me time to get acquainted with the children's mother. Her name is Gwyneth Pritchard. She has a becoming face and gray eyes and wears her hair curled and pulled back from her face. It's puffed at her crown but knotted full and loose and three short ringlets fall at the nape of her neck. When I called her "Mrs. Pritchard," she said, "Please, my friends call me Gwen."

"My friends call me Pringle," I told her. "Pringle

Duncan." (It's not a lie. My full name is Priscilla Duncan Rose, after my mother's side of the family.)

"Pringle Duncan it is," said Gwen.

Oh! The Erie train whistle! Must catch Gideon and Mozie.

ON BOARD THE ERIE TRAIN
1:45 P.M.

Gwen and I are sitting together in the ladies' compartment. Mozie is safely tucked inside the carpetbag, purring contentedly. Lucy is petting Mozie.

Two more women boarded at Binghamton. They began to sit across from us, then looked at Gideon and moved two rows back. The older woman has white, white hair pulled elegantly into a low knot at the nape of her neck. She is draped in a solid black dress made of fine silk. Her younger companion is wearing a rose-colored dress with a ruffled skirt headed with two bands of black velvet and trimmed with black Spanish lace. She has great twists of dark hair that circle her head, top and back.

TWO DAYS SLOW

On the train home from Merrywood, Uncle Edward sat next to me. How I wished I could shut up like a telescope! My uncle pretended to read, but in the window glass, I could see him studying me. His mouth twitched, as if he were practicing the words to console me.

In Scranton, the train wheels screamed to a stop, metal on metal. The conductor rushed to set the steps in place. I scanned the crowd for Father, who always greeted me when I returned home. I caught myself and felt a fresh stab of pain. Why does grief trick the heart so?

Uncle Edward brushed off the sleeves of his black waistcoat. "The coming days will not be easy, Pringle. We'll do the best we can." He took my hand and helped me step down to the platform. His hand felt fat and fleshy and did not convey the strength and assuredness that Father's always did.

A scrawny boy offered to drag my trunk to a cab, but my uncle waved him off, not even offering a single copper penny, and dragged the trunk himself. *Hire someone who can do a job as well as you can.* That's what Father always said.

Somehow I forced my legs to work, to set one numb foot in front of the other. Each step felt like a dream. Why did Scranton look the same? My whole world had turned upside down. Shouldn't the city have changed? Draped itself in black?

As I reached the cab, someone called, "Miss! Miss!"

A young man was calling to me. He was wearing a plug hat and yellow duster. His dark hair was parted in the middle and combed smoothly away from his face. He had a long, bright red cut on his cheek and eyes the color of a storm.

Why did I notice these things? I don't know.

"You dropped this," he said, handing me a red bound book with gilt lettering.

My heart swelled with gratitude. It was *Alice's Adventures in Wonderland.*

I clutched the book to my heart. I could barely speak. How close I had come to losing Mother's gift, which she had inscribed, *"To my darling Pringle, everything's got a moral, if only you can find it."*

“Thank you,” I murmured.

Alice’s rescuer lifted his hat, and walking backward, said, “Pardon me, miss. I’m in a hurry and my watch is two days slow.”

He spun on his heel and took off, coattails flying.

Two days slow. What a curious thing to say! Uncle Edward helped me into the hired carriage and rapped on the hood, signaling the livery driver. It wasn’t until the carriage lurched forward that I looked at the book in my lap and remembered the White Rabbit had said the very same thing to Alice.

MARTIAL LAW

The closer the horse trotted toward home, the bigger and darker the hollow feeling grew inside me. I wanted the carriage ride to stretch an eternity. The longer the ride, the more possible that Mother and Father were still alive and I’d never land at the bottom of that deep well.

On street corners, soldiers milled about. “The city’s under martial law,” said my uncle.

I knew. Father had written about the strike in his letters. One week ago, Good Friday, the striking miners had rioted, setting fire to a breaker. As if they had the right to destroy personal property!

And that wasn't all. The miners attacked and terrorized scab workers who quit the strike and returned to work. They shot off their guns at all hours. Our governor sent soldiers to protect the city and its citizens and their personal property.

The carriage halted in front of my house, where a large black wreath draped the front door. As I climbed the stone steps, our manservant waited in the open door. Jenkins has worked for our family as long as I can remember. Swallowing hard, he said, "I'm sorry for your loss, Miss Pringle."

Our housekeeper stood behind him. Mrs. Goodwin is a mighty barrel of a woman. I threw my arms around her and sobbed. She wrapped her meaty arms around me and said, "There, there."

"That will be all, Mrs. Goodwin," said a voice so crisp the edges crumbled off the words. "Priscilla needs her family now."

It was Aunt Adeline. She looked like a famished

blackbird in her mourning garb. She held out her arms to me. "My dear niece," she said, "life has dealt you a terrible blow."

Standing next to her was my cousin Ellen, who is nine and despicable. Her pale eyes roved over my face, as if plumbing the depth of my sorrow. "I'm sorry for your loss."

I ignored my aunt's open arms. "Where's Gideon?" I said.

"Upstairs," said Ellen.

Ellen skipped after me, but I spun around, saying, "I wish to be alone with my brother."

"Mama?" said Ellen.

"Let Pringle be," said Uncle Edward.

"Honestly, Edward," my aunt said, "there's no harm if Ellen wants to—"

"Let her be," repeated my uncle, which was unusual because Aunt Adeline is not a woman to oppose.

I gulped back a sob as I gripped the banister. The last time I'd seen Mother on those stairs, she was dressed for a holiday party. Her black hair was piled on her head. Soft ringlets framed her face. Her green crinoline gown made her eyes shine like green glass. Father had stood at the bottom of the staircase, looking up at her with keen admiration.

When I reached the carpeted hall, I whistled for Gideon, two high notes and one low. It's a game we invented when we played hide-and-seek in our garden.

I listened for his whistle – two low and one high – and the flat-footed way he slaps his feet when he runs.

Silence.

I started down the hall and paused outside Mother's bedroom. I whistled again. This time I heard a soft sound, as if someone were blowing through a straw.

I opened the bedroom door. Mother's room was dark, its long damask curtains drawn. My mouth went dry at the lingering scent of her jasmine and violet perfume. I wet my lips and whistled again.

From inside her dressing room came Gideon's almost whistle. I pulled open the double doors, and there sat Gideon, cross-legged. Mother's gowns were whorled like a nest around him. He clutched Mozie and wouldn't look at me.

"I'm here." I cupped his chin in my hand, forcing him to look at me. "Did you hear me?"

He pressed his lips together tightly.

"Gideon, say something, please."

"That's the way he's been." It was Mrs. Goodwin. "Master Gideon hasn't spoken one word since the accident. Something's wrong, terribly wrong."

"What is that creature doing in there?" It was Aunt Adeline.

I popped to my feet, ready to light into my aunt, who often referred to my brother by horrible names as if he weren't even a person with feelings. Then I realized she was talking about Mozie.

"Gideon was hiding the cat in Aunt Eliza's closet," said Ellen.

"You lie," I said.

Ellen's lower lip trembled. Anger flashed over Aunt Adeline, but she smoothed her features. "I know you're grieving, Pringle, but sorrow is no excuse for incivility."

I scooped up the cat. From the way he furled and unfurled his claws, I could tell Mozie was thinking terrible things about my aunt.

This is what you need to know about Mozie. He never forgets a slight, no matter how small.

THE ETIQUETTE OF GRIEF

I led Gideon to his room and told him to get washed and dressed for bed. No sooner had I finished dressing for bed, than Aunt Adeline came to my room. "You might find this helpful," she said, setting a book on my dresser. "Now get your dresses ready for the dye pot."

Once her footsteps tapped down the hall and her bedroom door clicked shut, I snatched up the book. It was an etiquette book. A black ribbon marked the chapter on mourning. With shaking hands, I opened to the marked page.

The mourning period for a mother or father lasts one year, it said. Six months of first or deep mourning, and six months of second mourning.

My thoughts became stinging arrows.

How long for a mother *and* a father? Two years? Should I mourn two parents concurrently or each in tandem, and if so, whom do I mourn first?

Or perhaps I should alternate the days, one day for Mother and the next for Father, or divide the days, the morning for Mother and the evening for Father.

I flipped through the pages. For the first six months, I was restricted to the simplest dress of solid black wool trimmed with crepe, a black crepe bonnet with black crepe facings and black strings – absolutely no hat – and a black crepe veil. No kid leather gloves, only those cut from black cloth, silk, or thread. No embroidery, jet trimmings, puffs, plaits, or trimming of any kind, and for the first month, no jewelry.

The next three months, I could wear black silk with crepe trimming, white or black lace collar and cuffs, a tulle veil and white bonnet-facings. The last three months, I may wear gray, purple, and violet.

I snapped the book shut and heaved open my

trunk. I pulled out my dresses and petticoats and stockings for the dye pot. I hid my favorite blue dress in the back of my closet.

THERE BUT FOR THE GRACE OF GOD

Lucy is an ornery child. Each time her mother took a nibble of corn bread or bite of apple or closed her eyes for a moment's rest, Lucy tormented Adam, poking him or kicking him or making faces.

Nearby, Mrs. Duggan and her daughter-in-law sniffed and looked down their noses at Gwen. They nodded smugly and looked at one another, telegraphing a secret message between them.

By the by, the Duggans asked Gwen where she was traveling, and when she said, "Chicago," they exclaimed and raised their hands to their mouths and twittered like birds, because they lived in Chicago.

They are the sort of women who pretend to be interested and pepper you with questions so that they have an excuse to talk about themselves.

The older Mrs. Duggan told about her family

and her late husband's family and her ever-so-intelligent son and how both sides of her family were from a long line of important So-and-Sos and all the fine things they do and all the fine parties they attend and all the fine things they own in their fine houses.

I pretended to admire all the things they said, but in my head, I rattled off things about my own family that would make them stop winking their eyes and smiling at each other and thinking they are the finest women in the car.

Then the older Mrs. Duggan said, "My grandson attends Harvard. Top of his class, he is. Do you know what Harvard is, dear?"

Gwen said, "That's nice" and "How proud you must be!" Then she began to say something about her own husband, but the older Mrs. Duggan interrupted her, saying, "It was nice talking with you, dear," which was funny because she and her daughter-in-law had done all the talking. It was clear that the Mrs. Duggans had grown bored with us because they had nothing more to say to impress us.

The younger Mrs. Duggan wagged her head and clucked sympathetically at Gideon. "There but for the grace of God go I. That's what it says in the Bible, you know."

"The Bible says no such thing," I retorted.

"Oh, my," said Mrs. Duggan. "Is that what they teach in colliery schools?"

A colliery school! Merrywood is no colliery school, and it's in Philadelphia, not Scranton. I bit my tongue. The Duggans are the sort of women my mother called foolish.

GIDEON

This is what I want the Mrs. Duggans and everyone else to know about my brother: Gideon is ten years old and a good boy and doesn't have a mean bone in his body, but some people are mean to him because he is different.

Some people are afraid of Gideon, as if he has a contagious disease or might hurt them. Some people feel sorry for Gideon because they think he has had misfortune to be born the way he is. That's why people like Mrs. Duggan say foolish things like, "There but for the grace of God go I," as if God has favored her or has been watching over her and taken care of her and not Gideon.

Well, God watches over Gideon, too.

It's true that Gideon isn't like other children his age. He doesn't look like other children, either. He is shorter than most boys his age and has a moon face and almond eyes that are slightly crossed and a flat nose and stubby fingers.

The doctors have theories about children like Gideon. They say children like him cannot live normal lives. That they cannot contribute to society and be responsible. That they will grow up to be criminals. That they should live in special places.

That's why you don't see children like Gideon. Most mothers don't keep babies like Gideon. The babies are whisked off to orphanages and never spoken about again.

Mother said those doctors and their theories could go to thunder. She believed the work of God is displayed through children like Gideon and that they have great potential.

Little by little, Mother taught Gideon his numbers and the alphabet and now he can read simple words and sentences and do simple math. He loves to count! Schoolwise, he is just a few years behind other children his age.

In most ways, Gideon is just like other children. He is happy-go-lucky. He can be as talkative – and argumentative – as a blue jay. He loves to run and romp and play.

Gideon has two moods: thunderstorm and sunshine. When he smiles, he smiles with his whole face, and when he laughs, his whole body laughs. He has feelings and they get hurt, just as mine do.

Gideon has very clean habits. He is obedient and well mannered and has a puffed-up sense of self-importance, which shows when he walks or learns something new, such as telling time or tying his shoes. He is unbearable when he learns something I don't know. If there's a bird nest or a litter of kittens or puppies or a nest of baby bunnies, Gideon will find it.

That brings me to his one bad habit: bringing

home stray dogs. The last dog he brought home was a collie. The dog was neatly brushed and knew how to sit and shake hands, and when its master knocked on our door, Father said, "Gideon, this must stop."

A PILLAR OF SALT

Gideon wanted to walk by himself to the men's washroom. I forbade it because he must cross to the men's compartment. Angry! Gideon folded his arms over his chest and tucked his hands in his armpits and glowered at me. He doesn't like to be treated like a baby.

I would not give in. I ignored the looks from the men passengers and stood outside the men's washroom door. Inside I heard splashing and then a man said, "Hey, kid, are you taking a bath?"

That Gideon! When he washes, he scrubs his hands, front and back, all the way to his elbows, and his neck and ears, with soap and water, just as Mother taught him. When Gideon emerged, he was shiny pink and his hair was slicked to the side and his shirt was soaked.

We returned to the ladies' compartment, where I waited my turn. The toilet room is a cramped, airless closet. The toilet is a wooden box with a round hole, nothing more than an outhouse on wheels. It's frightening to look down the toilet hole and see the iron rails and wooden tracks moving beneath. But the rumbling of the wheels means we're moving forward.

Father always said there's no turning back in life, no matter how hard you wish it. There is only moving forward, and you must not settle for the past or the present but must always look to tomorrow. "Look what happened to Lot's wife," Father would say. "Who wants to be a pillar of salt?"

Why do I look back, then? Our bodies are composed of skin and bones and muscle and sinew, but our minds are composed of pieces of the people we love. That's why I look back, to put the pieces – the thoughts and feelings and memories – together in order to make sense out of everything.

For days after the funeral, nothing felt real. Each crack of the floorboard, each creak of the stair tricked my heart into thinking Father or Mother was walking down the hall. Then I'd remember and a dark feeling would spread through me and I'd feel the loss all over again.

Now I can see that I was still falling and my world was still spinning. I could only think, "Why me?" and "Why did God answer Jabez's prayer and not mine?" And to tell the truth, I still wonder these things.

BEST-LAID SCHEMES

I don't remember what people said at the funeral. I only remember that they came.

Over the days that followed the funeral, I couldn't make the simplest decisions and felt grateful that I didn't have to choose which dress or shoes to wear. I only had to pull a black dress from my closet.

Father quoted the Scottish poet Robert Burns when his plans went awry. "'The best-laid schemes o' Mice an' Men,'" he'd say. "'Gang aft agley, An' lea'e us nought but grief an' pain, For promis'd joy!'"

But no matter how many plans went awry, Father was never despondent or sad. Nor did he give up.

One day, as I passed Father's library, his chair exhaled a familiar sigh. My heart sang out, for there was Father sitting at his gleaming walnut desk.

The figure shifted. Father disappeared, and in his place sat Uncle Edward. His hair, the shape of his head, his eyes and nose – they were similar to Father's.

My heart had tricked me again. My heart saw what it wanted to see, not what was true and real.

Know this: Edward Rose is no Franklin Rose. The two men are as different as night and day. Father was strong and a man of conviction and principle who never wavered; he was either hot or cold. Edward was lukewarm and always saw the gray middle of a problem. That's why they never got along.

Ellen was perched on her father's lap, her arms twined around his neck as she chattered about a new doll.

"Of course, dear," said Uncle Edward. "I'll see what I can do."

He picked up Father's brass letter opener and sliced open an envelope. He slid out the letter and his brow furrowed as he looked over its contents.

"Who's Dr. van Lavender, Papa?"

"A family friend of your mother's." He folded the letter and dropped it into his satchel.

Ellen pointed a pudgy finger at me. "Pringle's spying on us."

"What an imagination you have! Pringle's not spying," said Uncle Edward. He kissed the top of her head and shooed her off his lap. "Run along, precious, so that I may talk with Pringle."

Ellen pouted, sticking out her lower lip, a habit she thinks makes her look adorable. It makes her look like a baboon.

She tightened her grip around her father's neck, but he pried her loose and scooted her toward the door.

"Off with your head," I whispered.

She stuck out her tongue.

Uncle Edward gestured to me, bidding me

to enter—as if I needed permission to enter my father's office!

"Such a dramatic child," he said about Ellen. "Her mother worries she'll want a life in theater."

It was maddening the way he excused Ellen's spoiled behavior.

The chair squeaked as Uncle Edward leaned back. "These days have been a strain," he said.

He gestured to a stack of paperwork. "Nearly every day brings another arson, more rocks hurled at men who quit the strike, and more men attacked on their way home from work."

The dark, puffy circles beneath his eyes aged him. He looked ready to give up.

"Father would never capitulate to the miners," I said. "If they want higher wages, they should seek work elsewhere."

My uncle suppressed a smile. "You have your father's head for business."

He laced his fingers together and studied his folded hands. "Pringle, it's no secret that your father and I didn't get along. We disagreed on many things. I always thought we'd have a lifetime to set things right between us, but we didn't. But there's one thing we did agree on." His eyes met mine. "I have some good news that will ease your mind."

My heart lifted. Were my uncle and aunt and cousin leaving? Good riddance. I would help them pack myself. I envisioned myself standing on the front porch, waving a handkerchief as their carriage rattled down the street. At last my life could return to normal, whatever normal was.

"I've been appointed guardian," said Uncle Edward.

"Whose guardian?" I asked.

Uncle Edward gave me the most curious look. "Why, your guardian. Yours and Gideon's."

A nail driven through my heart!

"Your aunt and I have always wanted more children," he said. "She's never gotten over losing little Eddie, you know."

My hands began to jump involuntarily. I clasped them to keep them still. "I don't need a guardian. I'm fourteen. I'm at the top of my class. I can manage a household and take care of Gideon."

"The law says otherwise."

"The law! The property law gives women the right to inherit property. I have the right to inherit my father's estate."

"That's true," said my uncle, pressing his fingertips together. "But you cannot manage it until you become of age."

A second nail!

"You needn't worry," said my uncle. "Your inheritance is held in a trust, for when you turn twenty-one. In the meantime, you can have faith that I'll do what's best for you and your brother."

Tears blurred my eyes. Not tears of sadness. Tears of hot anger. How dare Uncle Edward think he knew what was best for Gideon and me. He scarcely knew us.

I stormed out of Father's office and whorled around my bedroom like a tornado. I threw open my closet door. Everything was black. Black dresses, black petticoats, black stockings and slippers.

Nothing was blacker than my thoughts. I wanted someone to blame. I blamed my uncle and aunt and cousin as I tore each black dress from its hanger. I blamed Mother and Father as I bunched the dresses together. I blamed God as I pressed them to my face and screamed into the pile.

I know Aunt Adeline suffered terribly when little Eddie drowned, only three years old. She has never recovered. None of us have. Little Eddie was a sweet, loving, adorable child. But Gideon and I would never belong to Uncle Edward and Aunt Adeline.

My bedroom door creaked open. There stood Ellen. "Why are you crying?" Then her eyes widened as she looked at the dresses strewn over the floor. "Mama doesn't like an untidy house."

I knuckled the tears from my eyes. "Get out. It's my house. Mine and Gideon's."

I leaped at her and pinched her, hard.

Tears sprang to her eyes. Her mouth puckered. I expected Ellen to bawl to her mother, but she didn't.

A PLACE TO CRY

Our train stopped in Corning at six forty-five. I hungered for a proper meal with cloth-covered tables and a menu at the Dickinson Hotel, just two doors down from the station, but Gideon and I shared our cheese and bread and sausages.

At Merrywood, whenever I felt overwhelmed with studies and examinations, I sneaked away and hiked to the top of the bluff behind the chapel. The path was windy and steep and narrow. Everyone needs a private place to cry, and the bluff was mine.

I had no safe place now. Not my house. Not my bedroom. My parents weren't even buried one month, and each day Aunt Adeline packed up more of Mother's and Father's belongings and instructed Jenkins to carry the boxes to the attic.

Little by little, Aunt Adeline filled our house with her belongings, shipped up from their house in Wilkes Barre. Every table and bureau and windowsill was covered with tasteless knickknacks and potted plants and framed photographs of people I didn't know. The walls were covered with even more tasteless ornamental plates.

Aunt Adeline's prized possession was a clay-and-plaster sculpture called *The Foundling*, designed by a man named John Rogers. The statuette depicts a young woman handing over her baby to a man standing behind the door to an orphanage.

Mother and I had seen the brown or gray plaster statues in every art and bookstore window, whether we visited Scranton, Philadelphia, or New York City. Women seem determined to collect as many as they could. As soon as a new Rogers group becomes available, newspaper reporters herald it as a major event and women rush out to buy it.

Once, I asked Mother why we didn't own a Rogers group. She scoffed and called them sentimental decorations, not true art.

I'm glad Mother didn't see Aunt Adeline's statuary, and not because it's one more tasteless decoration. *The Foundling* makes me think about children like Gideon who are whisked off to orphanages, where they never see their families again.

A RIDE ALONG RIDGE ROW

The next weeks brought more riots by the striking miners. Scarcely a day passed in April and May that didn't bear news of another beating or attack on a man who dared to return to work in order to feed his family.

After nearly a month of confinement, I feared that I'd lose my mind if I didn't get out of the house. I told Jenkins, "I wish to ride along Ridge Row."

He faltered. "I don't think that's a good idea, Miss Pringle."

But I insisted, and so he did. As the carriage clattered along the road that ran like a spiny backbone high above Roaring Brook, I mettled myself, for it was the road that Mother and Father had ridden that warm spring morning.

What drew me there? Why do we torture ourselves by visiting and revisiting sites of painful remembrances? I don't know.

I imagined Father driving fast, the reins in his hand. Mother laughing and calling, "Faster, Franklin! We want to feel the wind against our faces." I imagined Father snapping the reins, urging the horse; Gideon laughing, yelling, "Go go go!" He loved a fast ride as much as Mother.

And then what?

Father was an expert driver and horseman. What caused the carriage to tip?

I rapped on the carriage hood. "Stop," I told Jenkins. I stepped from the carriage and stared down the steep drop to the brook. Water tumbled over great jutting rocks. My stomach turned over. Something sour inched its way up my throat. How many times had the carriage flipped before it landed upside down in the water?

The man who had discovered the accident came to the funeral. He wore the soft, worn clothing of a workingman, and he clutched his cap between his hands. Perhaps the buggy hit a rut, he said. Perhaps the wheel fell off. Perhaps the horse spooked and bolted, making my father lose control.

No one knew for sure. The only certainty was that the buggy had plunged over the steep embankment, taking my parents with them. Miraculously, Gideon had fallen out near the top.

Thoughts, feelings, memories, questions—they all lumped together in my throat. I swallowed hard to loosen them. I rapped again on the carriage hood, saying, "Jenkins, please take me to the cemetery."

From Ridge Row, we crossed Jefferson Avenue and drove up the broad Lackawanna Avenue. As we crossed the river, I spotted Father's breaker, a gloomy structure that rose a short distance down the river. No clouds of coal dust plumed the air. It sat idle, its workers on strike.

At the top of the hill, the carriage turned onto Main Street. Hyde Park was just a short ride from my house, but it might have been another country. The houses were tiny and cramped and run-down. They sat one after the other, like a row of broken teeth. It was Sunday, and the streets were filled with children, running, playing, chasing each other and screaming happily.

The carriage pulled up to the iron cemetery gate on Washburn Street. Jenkins offered to accompany me, but I said no, that I wished to be alone.

I followed the winding gravel path, past the graves of the Welsh miners killed in the Avondale accident two years ago, all the way to the small rise where my parents lay.

There was no headstone or monument. It would be placed on the first anniversary of their death. I pressed my cheek against the ground and sobbed.

TWO DAYS LATE (AGAIN!)

As I cried a pool of tears deep enough to drown in, a shadow fell over me. "Are you all right, miss?" asked someone.

I looked up, blinking in the sunlight. It was a young man, a few years older than I, perhaps sixteen or seventeen. I bristled at his poor manners! How dare he intrude upon a mourner paying her respects. "I'm fine," I said.

He reached out to help me stand, but I ignored his hand. As I stood, my foot caught my petticoat, ripping its hem and pitching me forward. I landed on my knees.

In a single, flowing movement, he shot out a hand and caught me. His hand was rough and had a quiet strength.

"After a fall such as that," he said, "you shall think nothing of tumbling down stairs. How brave they'll all think you at home!"

It was the very thing Alice had said, after her fall down the rabbit hole! Oh, this boy's laughing gray eyes and grinning face! Didn't he think he was clever! Of all the bad manners! To poke fun at someone wearing a mourning dress!

"'Why, I wouldn't say anything about it,'" I retorted, "'even if I fell off the top of the house!'" Which is very true and the very thing that Alice had said after her great fall.

Was he ashamed? No. He had no shame. He laughed.

Was there no end to his coarseness? The familiar way he looked at me! As if he knew me!

I glared at him, taking in his medium height, his slight build, his dark hair, and thin, pink scar on his cheek. His striped shirt and its heavy collar were fresh and clean but his trousers and cap were the common clothing of a worker.

But, of course he knew me. He worked in the mines. Every mineworker knew my father and knew about the accident.

That realization made his bad manners inexcusable. I have no patience for coarse boys. I swished off toward the waiting carriage.

"I wish you wouldn't be so easily offended!" he called after me. "Come back! I've something important to say." And then, as I hurried through the cemetery gate, "'Well, be off, then!'"

It didn't matter how many lines from *Alice* he tossed after me. I climbed into the carriage and pulled the door shut. "Home, Jenkins," I said.

With each lurch of the carriage, something ticked like a clock in my head, except, instead of ticking forward, it tocked back to where I'd seen that grinning, impertinent face before. He was the same young man who had rescued Alice at the train station and returned her to me. That day, he wore a yellow duster and the cut on his cheek was red and raw. That day he had said his watch was two days late, just like the White Rabbit.

And now, here he was again.

My mouth twitched and spread into a grin for the first time in a very long time, and it felt good. Of course, I scolded myself soundly.

This train is stingy with its lighting—just six candles for our car. It's growing too dark to write. I'll close here and try to sleep, though sleep is impossible when I recall that grinning face.

TUESDAY, SEPTEMBER 5, 1871
BUFFALO, NEW YORK
8:30 A.M.

MISS RINGWALD'S LETTER

The train arrived in Buffalo at 7:20 this morning. Tired! My legs had turned to sea legs. At a clean-looking inn, we filled ourselves with eggs and ham and thick toast slathered with strawberry jam. Lucy spit out the pits from her stewed prunes onto Adam's plate. Then Gideon showed Adam and Lucy how to hang a spoon from the ends of their noses. (It was a trick that Father taught Gideon.)

We walked to the Lake Shore & Michigan Southern station on Exchange Street, where we must wait until noon for the Lake Shore train. Gideon keeps taking out his pocket watch and checking the time. I told him it won't make the train come faster and to put the watch away or I'll take it from him until we reach Miss Ringwald's.

At Miss Ringwald's name, Gideon brightened. He dug through my carpetbag until he found her letter. How could a plain piece of rose-colored stationery mean so much? It's our ticket to a new life.

With his elbow, Gideon nudged me again until I agreed to read the letter once more. What a pest he can be!

This is what Miss Ringwald wrote:

My darlings,

I was crushed—crushed!—when I learned of the loss of your mother and father! How difficult this time must be for you and Gideon!

When I think of your mother, I think of our days together at Merrywood. We were young and as happy as larks! Trouble comes soon enough, my dear child. Enjoy life whenever you can!

Your mother and I enjoyed our school days. Did you know the switching our headmistress gave us when we climbed the bluff behind the chapel? (Of course, that didn't stop us!)

How proud your mother was of you and Gideon! In each letter, she told me of your many accomplishments and your great potential!

Remember this: No matter how much pain you feel, there is something inside you that's stronger than the pain. In the coming days ahead, you must draw on your mother's courage and strength! (There was never a braver woman than your mother!)

How I wish I could be with you! If only so many miles did not separate us!

May God bless you and Gideon during this time and always!

Beatrice Ringwald

I like Miss Ringwald's large, loopy handwriting and the great flourishing strokes of her capital letters. This is what my name would look like in her handwriting:

Priscilla Rose

I like Miss Ringwald's exclamation marks! too! because they make everything! she! writes! look! so! passionate! and! exciting!!!!

I tucked the letter away. From the bottom of the carpetbag, I pulled out Mother's red cloak and draped it over Gideon and me.

As we huddled, I told Gideon the story of our great-grandmother Annabella Duncan, and how she spun the wool from the fleece of Lord Duncan Abbot's finest sheep. Its stitches, so tiny and perfect, look as though a fairy sewed them with a silver needle.

When I wear the cloak, I am as strong and brave as my mother and grandmother and great-grandmother. That's what I told Gideon.

YOUR EYES, SIR

Miss Ringwald is Mother's favorite friend from their school days. She is a tiny woman, as bright as a firefly, who sleeps late every morning and refuses to wear a corset or hoop skirt. She wears drawers tied with ribbons around her ankles and often dresses in a *robe de chambre* in the afternoon.

"Beatrice," Mother would beg when she visited us, "this is Scranton, not Chicago," and "Please don't stand on the porch dressed like that."

Some women would say things like "Little pitchers have big ears," which was a secret code that meant adults should be mindful of what they say around children.

But not Miss Ringwald! She never told if I eavesdropped, never let on when I hid under the dining room table.

One night I spied from between the staircase spindles. Miss Ringwald was sitting in our parlor, one arm draped over the back of the divan, and talking to my mother, saying, "And so, Eliza, at a party a gentleman said to me, 'Madam, if I were to walk into your chamber and find you undressed, what part would you cover first?'"

My mother gasped. "Beatrice! He's no gentleman! Surely you didn't answer!"

Beatrice's laugh was one hundred silver thimbles. "Of course, I did. I said, 'Your eyes, sir! That's the part I'd cover first.'"

My mother and Beatrice collapsed into giggling fits on the divan.

Mother sat up and dabbed at her eyes. "Do you think you'll ever marry, Beatrice?"

"Pshaw!" said Miss Ringwald, dismissing the idea with a wave of her hand. "I see no need for marriage, unless I find a man who deems me equal in all things and who likes cats."

The rest of the weekend, all my mother or Beatrice had to say was, "Your eyes, sir," and they would giggle like schoolgirls. Father said, "What's wrong with my eyes?" And then, hearing them laugh, he would stare and them and ask, "Have you ladies been nipping the sherry?"

Father liked to say, "God helps those who help themselves," but Miss Ringwald said, "God helps those who can't help themselves."

Miss Ringwald's mission was the humane society. She wrote letters to newspapers and state legislators, urging them to enact laws to protect animals from cruel owners. She led boycotts against horse companies that neglected or abused their animals. She lectured on the evils of blood sports such as dog and rooster fighting and animal baiting.

She formed a patrol to prevent and punish animal abuse. Once, she performed a citizen's arrest of two men who were dragging a frightened, squealing pig through the streets to the slaughterhouse.

"Each time my name is printed in the newspaper, it embarrasses my father," she confessed to Mother.

"There was that pistol incident," said Mother.

"It was a warning shot!" said Miss Ringwald. "And well over his head! Honestly, Eliza, if you saw the way that driver flogged his horse! The dray was too heavy for the poor thing."

She sniffled. "Father took away my pistol. He says as long as I live in his house, I must abide by his rules and I must do something about the cats."

"Twenty-six is quite a few," said Mother.

Miss Ringwald sniffled again. "It boils down to a difference of religion."

Mother looked shocked. "Are you no longer a Presbyterian?"

"I've converted," said Miss Ringwald brightly. "I'm a Saint Bernard."

12:30 P.M.

At long last we have boarded the Pacific Express, the Lake Shore & Michigan Southern train that will carry us to Miss Ringwald's Chicago!

The sun is shining brightly and the sky is the clearest blue with piles of white clouds, reminding me how far we've traveled from Scranton's clouds of black coal dust.

Our carriage is crowded with women dressed in steel-plate fashion, as *Godey's Lady's Book* would say. The women look as fine and finer than the two Mrs. Duggans.

One woman is wearing violet silk and a skirt trimmed with six narrow ruffles. She has a kind face and yellow hair. She bumped into Gideon as she boarded. She apologized profusely and patted his head and gave him a lemon drop.

Just as the conductor passed through our carriage to punch our tickets, the woman in the violet dress slid from her seat and headed toward the washroom. The conductor scowled at her empty seat and wrote a note to himself.

She took a very long time in the washroom, and when she seated herself again, the conductor had already passed through. Lucy is standing on her seat, watching the woman intently. "Your eyebrow is missing," said Lucy.

She hurried back to the washroom. The woman's eyebrows are painted on!

LATER

I don't know what's gotten into Adam and Sallie. Usually it's Lucy who misbehaves, but Adam assailed the seat cushions, punching them, sending up clouds of dust.

Then, without provocation, Sallie sank her teeth into Adam's shoulder. Adam screamed but Sallie had latched on and wouldn't let go, not when Gwen shook her (Adam screamed louder) and not when Gwen swatted her behind (Adam screamed even louder). Sallie sank her teeth deeper.

The woman in the violet dress tossed a tumbler of water into Sallie's face. The shock broke her hold. Sallie wasn't hurt, just surprised. Her wet little face puckered up and she cried.

Gwen smiled at the woman, embarrassed, but inside that smile was a set of clenched teeth. "Two days ago, she turned into a cannibal," said Gwen, mopping Sallie's face with a handkerchief.

"Bite her back," said the younger Mrs. Duggan.

"What kind of mother would do that?" said the woman in the violet silk. "Two wrongs don't make a right."

Young Mrs. Duggan huffed and went back to minding her own business.

Meanwhile, Gideon tugged frantically on my

sleeve. His pocket watch is missing. Adam and Lucy and I have searched everywhere, high and low. I fear he dropped it down the toilet hole and it's lying somewhere on the tracks.

I feel terrible. Why didn't I take the watch from him while I had the chance?

LATER

The conductor returned for the violet lady's ticket. As soon as she spotted him, she closed her eyes and pretended to be napping, but he leaned over and said, "Excuse me, madam. Your ticket, please?"

She awoke with a dramatic start. "My ticket? You frightened me half to death for a ticket?"

"Yes, ma'am."

Meanwhile, Lucy hugged the back of her seat, watching the woman fumble through her carpet-bag. "It's here someplace," said the woman. "You needn't lord over me. You must have other tickets to collect."

"Just yours, madam," said the conductor. "I don't mind waiting."

The further the woman dug through her bag,

the farther Lucy tipped herself for a better look. Suddenly, Lucy piped, "There's Gideon's pocket watch!"

All kindness evaporated from the woman's face. She snapped the carpetbag shut. "Shut your trap, kid."

The conductor hurried from the car and returned with a man wearing a uniform and a badge. He pawed through the woman's carpetbag. He found no ticket, but he did find Gideon's pocket watch. The woman was a stowaway and a thief! He arrested her immediately, and at the very next stop, he will escort her from the train.

Lucy beamed and puffed up with importance when the conductor praised her and called her a heroine. There will be no living with that child now.

TO LIVE IN A RABBIT HOLE

Lucy is the most exasperating and contrary child I have ever met! Just after we left Dunkirk, she began speaking in opposites. If her mother says yes, she says no. If her mother says up, she says down. If her mother says "Lucy," she says, "My name is Sallie." If her mother calls her "Sallie," Lucy changes the rules and says, "I'm not Sallie, I'm Adam."

One minute Lucy is happy and laughing. The next minute she is throwing herself against the seat cushions, whining, "I hate this train! I want to get off!"

To think we have nearly twenty more hours to go!

"I'll tell you a story," I said.

"Stories are stupid," she said as she climbed into my lap.

"Once upon a time," I began, "there were three little children and their names were Adam, Sallie, and Lucy—"

"No!" said Lucy. "I'm not last. Sallie's the baby. She goes last."

Lucy had a point. I started over. "Once upon a time there were three little children and their names were Adam, Lucy, and Sallie, and they lived at the bottom of a rabbit hole."

Lucy clapped her hands. "A rabbit hole! I should

like to live in a rabbit hole." Then a worried look crossed her face. "Except that a rabbit hole would be damp and dark because it's in the ground."

"Oh, but this rabbit hole is dry and snug," I told her.

Lucy furrowed her brow, thinking it over. "Dry and snug are good. But it's still dark."

"Rabbits have excellent eyesight," I said.

"How do you know?" said Lucy.

That was a good question. "Have you ever seen a rabbit wearing spectacles?"

Lucy chewed on that.

"This rabbit hole was dug beneath a garden," I told her. "All the rabbits have to do is reach up to the ceiling and pull out a carrot. Morning, noon, and night they eat carrots."

"I don't like carrots very much," said Lucy.

"Then you can't be a rabbit," said Adam.

"But I want to be a rabbit!" wailed Lucy.

"You can't be a rabbit," said Adam. "Rabbits like carrots."

Lucy slid off my lap and threw herself into the aisle and rolled around, kicking her legs and flailing her arms and crying because she couldn't be a rabbit because she didn't like carrots.

The stares from the other lady passengers! I heard words like "spanking" and "over my knee" and "my children never." The younger Mrs. Duggan sniffed and said something about giving that child something to cry about. Gwen shot her a scalding look that could singe eyebrows.

I wanted to pick Lucy up, but Gwen stopped me. "Ignore her. She's overtired. When she has a tantrum like this, Peter and I wager how long it lasts."

Adam guessed two days.

I guessed an hour.

Gwen guessed, "Forty-six seconds."

We all lost. Lucy wailed herself out in one minute, ten seconds. Exhausted, she curled up next to her mother and fell asleep. Later, when she woke up, she was the most cheerful child. Even the older Mrs. Duggan complimented her, saying, "Your eyes are beautiful."

Lucy reached up with her little hand, touched Mrs. Duggan's baggy neck, and said most sincerely, "Your chins are beautiful, too."

A RIDDLE

As Lucy napped, I thought about the boy at the cemetery and how the very next Sunday, bright yellow daffodils crowned a small jar at my parents' grave.

Inside the jar, standing among the green pipe stems, was a rolled piece of white paper. I fished it out. In a clear hand with sharp, angular lines and no curve, someone had written:

Dear Alice,

Why is a raven like a writing desk?

Rabbit

It felt as if sunshine had burst inside me.

Grinning, I wrote back:

Dear Rabbit,

Ask the Hatter or the March Hare.

Alice

P.S. You should have something better to do with your time than waste it asking riddles that have no answers.

Then I rolled the paper and tucked it back in the jar, feeling terribly mischievous and guilty. I knew what Mother would say, if she saw me writing a note to a boy.

But it felt delicious to have a secret. That night I wrote to Merricat, telling her about Alice's rescuer. I counted the days till Sunday, hoping to find another note.

FOREVER RABBIT AND FOREVER ALICE

Near the end of May, the strike ended and the miners straggled back to work. The very next Saturday, Mrs. Robson rushed home from marketing, terribly agitated. There had been an explosion in a West Pittston coal mine. Thirty-eight men and boys were trapped.

All of Scranton held its breath, praying for the trapped mine workers, but by the time rescuers reached the men, twenty had died. I prayed that Rabbit wasn't among the dead. If he were, how would I ever know? I didn't even know his real name.

The next two Sundays, I found no notes and no

fresh flowers. I poured out my heart to Merricat, telling her I felt more lonesome than any person can bear.

The second Sunday in June, Rabbit was waiting for me. Oh, his pride! "Happy to see me?" he said, falling into step as I walked down the gravel path.

A girl should never admit that she is happy to see a boy, but I admitted that the West Pittston coal mine disaster weighed on me. "The newspapers call it a second Avondale."

A shadow crossed his face and lingered there for a second. I looked at his hands. His fingernails bore the black lines of coal dust impossible to scrub away. Had he returned to work with the miners? Did he labor long hours underground, missing the sunlight, the scent of lilacs, the flight of a sparrow?

"Who are you?" I asked. "What is your name?"

The shadow had disappeared and his eyes were teasing again. "I might ask the same question," he said.

It would be a lie if he said he didn't know my

name. I had seen him studying me, searching my face, the flicker of recognition. I'm sure he saw my father's stubbornness in my chin and my mother's willful spirit in my wide eyes.

"'I knew who I was when I got up this morning,'" I said, "'but I've changed several times since then.'"

He laughed and took off his cap and slapped the dust from it. "Fair enough," he said. "Then you are forever Alice and I am forever Rabbit."

He looked at me intently. Under his gaze, something about him emerged into plainer view and lingered there for a second. There was something about him that felt dangerous and yet thrilled me at the same time. I tried to put my finger on it, but couldn't.

I looked away, toward the street where Jenkins waited patiently in the carriage, the horse flicking flies away with her tail. My legs felt a sudden urge to run to the safety of the carriage.

A TASTE OF LICORICE

Each Sunday night, I wrote to Merricat, filling pages about Rabbit. How we met each Sunday at the cemetery. How a jar full of fresh flowers – violets, daisies, whatever bloomed – marked my parents' graves. How we strolled the gravel path, past picnickers, some dressed in black, some in their Sunday best. How I was full of words, and happy to let them out. What did we talk about? Everything. Nothing.

Merricat asked if Rabbit was handsome. I wouldn't call him handsome, but there was something striking that made me catch my breath and chilled me even though the sun was warm. But never for long. At night, thoughts of Rabbit warmed me.

I told Merricat how one Sunday, when Rabbit leaned closer to me, my face grew hot and my heart quickened and I couldn't breathe. My hands turned clammy.

Will he, won't he, will he, won't he, will he kiss me?

I hoped so, I hoped not. Frightened, I pulled away.

For a brief second, something flashed like lightning in his eyes. What was it? Hurt, I think. Hurt that we came from different neighborhoods, lived in different worlds, had no business being together, and could never be together, except where grief had melded our worlds. What grief did he suffer? What sorrow did he bear? I don't know. He would never say.

Rabbit didn't understand, or perhaps he understood too well. He walked away, as if he hadn't a care. I wanted to cry after him to wait. I wanted to fly to him, but I didn't.

All the ride home, I felt as though I had folded into myself. I longed for Mother. I needed my mother. Would she understand? She and Father came from the same world, but it wasn't always that way, not for their parents and grandparents.

A girl must confide in someone, and so I wrote to Merricat that night, telling her how betrayed and hurt I felt. How could Rabbit leave me? How could he walk away? Why didn't he understand the risk I took to meet him?

I argued with myself! I was never going to the cemetery again. I was going. I didn't want to see him. I wanted to see him. I hated him. I longed for him.

Then came the next day—the 14th of August—and another terrible explosion that killed seventeen mine workers in the Eagle Shaft in Pittston. Day in and day out, I paced the floors with worry. How would I know if Rabbit was safe, if I didn't even know his name? I longed to talk with someone but had no one.

The next Sunday, the violets limped over the side of the jar. Loneliness and hurt and anger and self-pity and grief rolled together in my stomach in one hard lump.

Suddenly, Rabbit stepped out from behind a tall monument. His strong fingers gripped my arm. He had come. He pulled me behind the tall monument and my feet obeyed. Crying, I struck his chest with my fists. "You left me."

He didn't apologize. He ran his hand through my hair. The pins dropped and my hair fell loose about my shoulders. I leaned into him, despite myself. He cupped my face between his hands, and kissed me.

That night, with the gaslight turned low, I wrote to Merricat and told her that Rabbit's kisses taste like licorice.

I KNOW IT'S A SIN

Every few weeks, Uncle Edward traveled to Philadelphia on business. How I dreaded those days!

At tea one afternoon, Ellen said, "Mother, may I have a diary like Pringle's?"

I dropped my teaspoon. "You've been prying through my things! Have you no decency?"

Ellen's lower lip quivered. She started to cry, big sopping tears that rolled down to her chin. She had a talent for turning tears on and off. "I wasn't prying. I saw you writing in your diary."

Aunt Adeline glared at me. "Now look what you've done." Then to Ellen, she said, "Of course,

I'll buy you a diary, my sweet. When I was your age, I kept a diary." My aunt's eyes brimmed with tears as she recalled her mother. "Each night, my mother read my diary and wrote notes to me. If I couldn't think of something to write about, she provided suggestions. I promise to do the same for you."

My aunt went on to say that girls should write about the weather, visits with friends, and the books they've read. Girls should never indulge in fantasy or gossip.

"My mother said that the purpose of a diary is to record events," I said. "She believed that every woman's life is important and that we should write to make meaning out of our daily lives and our experiences."

"Nonsense," said Aunt Adeline. "A young lady should shine in the art of conversation, but not too brightly or no man will be interested in her."

I disagreed. "A young woman should be comfortable in the world of ideas. She should express herself in a thoughtful and logical manner."

My aunt's lips twitched, but before she could respond, Gideon belched. Loudly.

Aunt Adeline's eyes snapped! "Apologize," she said.

But Gideon didn't because he couldn't. He stared at his plate.

"I said, 'Apologize.'"

"He can't," I said. "He's mute."

"It's not that he can't," said Aunt Adeline. "He won't. He's a willful, spoiled child and he's refusing to talk to spite me. I will not abide a willful, spiteful child."

She threw her napkin on the table. Her chair grated against the floor as she stood. She circled around to Gideon and grabbed his arm. She yanked him from the table and upstairs.

A door slammed shut. "Apologize," yelled my aunt. A loud *thwack* followed. Again she yelled, "Apologize," and then came another sickening *thwack*.

I cried out and pushed away from the table so hard my chair toppled.

"Don't!" said Ellen. "You'll catch it next."

My only care was Gideon. The third blow came as I reached the stairs. I bounded up the steps, two at a time. The sound came again as I reached Gideon's door. It was locked.

I shouted and threw myself against the door. "Don't hit him! He doesn't understand!"

Mercifully, I didn't hear another blow. My aunt emerged, her eyes bright and her face flushed. In her hand, she held a leather strap. "Perhaps he understands now."

Gideon was curled in a ball on his bed, facing the wall. Four bright red welts crisscrossed his naked back. I lunged for the strap.

She whipped the strap out of my reach and struck me, hard, telling me never to interfere with her discipline and that she was teaching Gideon and me a lesson for our own good.

After three more blows, she stopped. "That was just half the lesson. If you speak one word to your uncle, I'll give both of you the other half."

Would she do it? Surely she would, the next time business took Uncle Edward out of town. I didn't care about myself, but I wouldn't chance hurting Gideon for fear he might disappear inside himself forever.

That night, I stayed with Gideon. The welts burned like fire. I couldn't sleep. I turned up the gas lamp, opened my diary, and listed every hateful thought that came to mind. I wrote the ugliest things I could about Aunt Adeline and Uncle Edward and Ellen. I wrote until my hand cramped and I couldn't write any more.

I had closed the diary and turned down the gas lamp when someone rapped on Gideon's door. It was Ellen.

"What do you want?" I said.

"I'm sorry," she whispered. "About Mama." And then, "I know it's a sin, but sometimes I hate my mother."

A TASTE OF LYE

After the whipping, Gideon vanished far inside himself, and I didn't know if he'd ever return. Sometimes he sat and stared, looking lonesome and sad. I tried wishing and praying and even whistled two high and one low to coax him out of hiding, but he didn't.

Somehow we needed to rebuild our lives so that we could learn to live without our parents. But how? I prayed for an answer, and one day the answer came to me. Gideon needed a routine, the sort of school routine he had with Mother.

Each morning, we sat in the nursery and pored over his lessons, just as he and Mother had done. By and by, as I read stories to him, he came back a little bit.

Presently, Ellen joined us, too. At first I felt wary, but soon I reveled in the change I saw in her. She was kind and helpful to Gideon.

As we worked on lessons, I realized how much I missed Merrywood and my studies and my teachers and classmates. I longed to see them. I longed to return to them. Would I ever have a normal life again?

One morning as Gideon sat with a book in his lap, he began to trail his finger across the sentences. Tears ran off my face sideways! Gideon remembered everything Mother had taught him. I hugged him and kissed him and said how happy

I was that he came back and would he please, please come back just a little bit more and say something?

I thought for sure he would talk, now that he was back. There were times when his mouth opened as if he were about to speak, but then he clamped it shut as if he suddenly remembered he mustn't. If I pushed, he disappeared inside himself, and then I'd have to work hard to reach him there and pull him back from behind whatever door closed in his mind.

One morning, Aunt Adeline stood in the doorway, watching Gideon glide his finger across a sentence. "Look at Gideon pretending to read," she said.

"Gideon isn't pretending," said Ellen emphatically. "He reads."

Aunt Adeline looked as if she had witnessed the Eighth Wonder of the World.

I gritted my teeth. My insides seethed with disgust, but I explained as politely as I could how Mother had taught Gideon to read. I told her Gideon was eight when he learned his first word, "cat." I described the explosion of understanding on his face as he looked from the word "cat" to Mozie and then back again. I told her how Mother and I hugged him and wept with joy.

"She taught him herself?" asked Aunt Adeline, as if Mother teaching Gideon herself was somehow beneath her. "There are schools where —"

"Mother said anyone who suggested that Gideon belonged in one of those schools could go to blazes."

Aunt Adeline's eyes narrowed. "I will not tolerate language unbecoming to a young lady." She grabbed my arm, hauled me to the washroom, and washed my mouth out with soap.

Later, Ellen said sorrowfully, "I can't do lessons with Gideon anymore. Mama says he'll hold me back in my development. She's going to hire a governess for me."

OUR TORMENTOR

Mozie is the best cat in the world, just like Alice's cat, Dinah. He's a capital one for catching mice. He would eat a bird as soon as look at it.

But Aunt Adeline despised Mozie, and Mozie despised Aunt Adeline. He hid under furniture and swiped at her. If she disturbed his nap, he hissed and growled at her. If he climbed to the top of the porch roof, he had no trouble getting down. He aimed for Aunt Adeline. If Aunt Adeline could, she would have gotten him executed.

When the deep mourning period expired for my aunt and uncle and cousin and no longer required that they wear solid black, Aunt Adeline ordered new dresses for herself and Ellen, sewn from fine purple silk with a bonnet and matching shoes.

I was to be trapped in black for three more months.

One Sunday, as we sat in church, Aunt Adeline sniffed. "What is that stench?" she whispered to Uncle Edward.

He sniffed all around and then bent over. When he straightened up, he made a face. "My dear, it's your new shoes."

Mozie had used her shoes for a toilet.

Her face grew so red, I feared for her blood

vessels. As soon as the service ended, she wheeled us out the door and into the carriage.

At home, she charged through the kitchen, grabbing a flour sack. She snatched Mozie from his afternoon nap on a parlor chair, dropped him in the sack, and held out the twisting, growling sack to Jenkins. "Drown him."

"No!" screamed Ellen, lunging after the sack.

"Have you no mercy!" I said.

Aunt Adeline handed the sack to Jenkins and flounced from the room.

Oh, how Mozie fought for his life! He battled that sack, pummeling it, ripping at it with his teeth and claws.

Jenkins held the sack at an arm's length. "Sir?"

"Give it to me," said Uncle Edward. He spilled the cat outside.

Mozie lit across the garden as if his tail were on fire.

From then on, Mozie slept and took his meals in the carriage house. One morning, I saw Gideon pacing up and down the alley, clearly agitated, tapping at the carriage house door and pressing his ear to the door. He wouldn't go inside.

I didn't understand until I heaved open the carriage house door and saw something that shook me from head to toe: Father's broken buggy with its splintered axle and missing wheel.

Gideon stood stone still in the doorway, his pants drenched. Gideon had peed his pants.

A DO NOT DISTURB MAMA DAY

During one of Uncle Edward's trips to Philadelphia, Aunt Adeline grew as twitchy as a cat by the afternoon. She sent Mrs. Goodwin to the druggist, with an order written on a piece of paper and sealed in an envelope, and then paced about the parlor.

A little while later, Mrs. Goodwin returned with the mail and a package wrapped in brown paper. Aunt Adeline pounced on the package. She tore it open, took out a small container, and tapped two pills—for her nerves, she said—into the palm of her hand. She gulped the pills with water. Then she took the letters and climbed the stairs. Her bedroom door clicked shut behind her.

"It's best we stay out of your aunt's way today," said Mrs. Goodwin.

Ellen called it a "Do Not Disturb Mama Day."

I was sitting quietly in my room, daydreaming about Rabbit and wishing for a letter from Merricat, when my bedroom door flew open.

Aunt Adeline charged in, her face purple with rage. She brandished a leather strop in her hand. "Do you know how I have sacrificed to make a home for you and to care for you and your brother?"

For a moment, I was stupefied. I couldn't speak. I felt glued to my chair. I didn't know where her rage came from.

Then my wits returned. "Aunt Adeline, you're not feeling well," I said, talking as I moved, trying to wend my way around her. "Let me call Mrs. Goodwin. She'll bring you some tea."

Before I could reach the safety of the hall, Aunt Adeline grabbed my arm, digging her nails into my skin. "I am responsible for your moral development, to make sure you are a good, obedient girl, one who doesn't shame her family and sully her family's name."

My aunt withdrew a stack of letters from her pocket. All addressed to Merricat.

My heart sank. "How did you get those?"

"Merricat's mother is a good, decent woman," said Aunt Adeline. "She has forbidden you to write to her daughter again. I'll teach you not to make a fool out of yourself and out of this family."

She raised the leather strap and brought it down on me, flogging me as one would flog a horse.

Mother always said that we must give words to terrible experiences because words release the power that the experiences have over us, but even as I write the words, I cannot release the shame and humiliation of that beating. I'm going to close this diary for now.

LATER

Four thirty. Our train stopped in Erie, Pennsylvania. It felt good to walk on the platform and stretch our legs, even if only for fifteen minutes. After we boarded again and the train started off,

I began a game with Lucy and Adam and Gideon that Father and I had played.

"I see something yellow," I said.

Adam and Lucy took turns guessing, squealing when they spotted the yellow slippers on a lady passenger. Gideon played with his eyes, searching out each color. After several rounds, Gideon tapped me, motioning that he needed the toilet.

I let him go alone. Several minutes later, he returned, his face shiny pink and his forearms wet from scrubbing. His hands were cupped and his eyes twinkled mischievously.

"Mouse," he said, uncupping his hands.

Out popped a mouse! The poor thing trembled down to its tail!

Lucy screamed and Adam screamed and Sallie screamed just because they screamed. The frightened little creature leaped from Gideon's hands and darted down the aisle, causing the women to scream and lift their feet.

On the floor, the carpetbag swelled and twisted. In a flash, Mozie clawed his way out and bounded after the mouse.

"No!" screamed Lucy, and she leaped after the cat.

Gideon bounded after Lucy.

Adam chased Gideon.

Sallie toddled after Adam, screaming happily, waving her arms in the air.

I couldn't scream. I couldn't move a muscle. I just stood there, my heart bursting and tears squirting from my eyes. Gideon spoke!

The conductor caught Mozie and carried the squirming cat back to us. "Is this your stowaway?" he said.

"No," said Gideon. "That's my cat!"

"Does he have a ticket?"

"No," said Gideon. "He's a cat."

"Any more trouble, and I'll have him arrested," said the conductor.

Gideon took Mozie from the conductor. "Don't arrest my cat! No more trouble. I promise."

Once Gideon makes a promise, he means it. "Be a good cat," said Gideon as he tucked Mozie into the carpetbag. "Or you'll go straight to jail."

Lucy cried because she wanted a pet mouse. To quiet her, I read her the "Mouse's Tail" from *Alice.*

Gideon's first word in nearly five months has worn everybody out and now

Gideon, Adam,
and Lucy
are curled,
fast asleep,
one atop
the other,
like a nest
of mice
and Mozie
is napping
in the
carpetbag.

Seven fifteen. We stopped in Cleveland for supper. We slurped down mussels and thin broth with Gwen and the children.

All during supper, Gideon talked a blue streak.

It seems as though all the words that he had stored up over the months poured out. He told Adam how he found Mozie, a tiny kitten that fit into his hand, beneath a neighbor's porch; how Mozie's fur looks like an M on his forehead; how Mozie is short for the composer Mozart; and how Mozie is the best cat in the world.

Gwen remarked that she saw me writing in my diary and declared that no girl ever wrote more. That made something grow and grow inside me, and that was my desire to spill everything out, from my parents' accident to Aunt Adeline to Cousin Ellen and the terrible thing that had made us run away.

But I didn't tell Gwen any of those things. It's too soon. I told her that my parents had died recently, and that we're going to live with a friend of my mother's.

"It's hard to lose someone you love," said Gwen.

I felt myself well up, but I didn't want to cry in front of Gwen and everyone else in the dining car. There are times I have an overwhelming need to talk about my mother and father. I looked at

Gwen and knew she would listen lovingly, but something inside held me back.

I dabbed my eyes on the back of my wrists and excused myself to use the washroom. Sallie reached her chubby arms toward me. "May I take her?" I asked.

Gwen said, "Of course."

Sallie leaned into my arms and dug into my sides with her little legs as if she were riding a horse. I pushed my grief aside and we whinnied past the uppity Mrs. Duggans.

Gwen is staring sorrowfully out the window. I am glad I didn't add to her sorrows, whatever they may be, by telling her mine. Her mind seems to be working on something deep.

A VISIT FROM A DOCTOR

One day, after a heavy August rain had scattered the petals from Mother's favorite rosebush, I was sitting in our garden, mourning the roses, when a visitor from Philadelphia called on us. Aunt Adeline introduced Dr. van Lavender as an old family friend.

His name sounded familiar, and then I recalled the letter Uncle Edward had received long ago. Dr. van Lavender was a tiny man with a pointy gray beard and clear blue eyes.

Mostly, he asked questions about Gideon. He said, "I see" a lot and scribbled my answers in a tiny notebook. His handwriting looked like a secret code.

He wanted to know about Mother's side of the family and if I had known my grandmother and aunts and girl cousins.

I said no, that I'd never met my grandmother, that she died when I was a baby and that I was the only daughter of an only daughter who was also an only daughter.

Dr. van Lavender marveled at that and wrote that down, too.

He asked me about Gideon and the sort of boy he was. I said, "Do you mean before the accident?" and he said, "Yes."

I answered Dr. van Lavender as honestly as I could. There was something about his demeanor that made me want to answer him. I told him that Gideon was backward in learning to walk and to talk and that it took him longer to learn some things, but that Mother always said there are a time and a season for everything, especially children, who are God's greatest creation.

The doctor nodded. "Your mother was a wise woman."

"Yes, she was!" I said. It felt so good to talk about Mother. I told him how Mother taught Gideon to read and to write and to do simple math and to tell time.

I told him how Gideon loved to play, just like other boys his age, even though he is clumsy and can't do everything as well they do, but he wants to keep up.

The doctor nodded and wrote down everything and wanted to know about Gideon's daily habits.

"Gideon has nice habits," I assured the doctor. "He's clean and takes care of all his personal needs. He washes himself exceedingly well and is very particular about his clothing, especially his shoes. He doesn't like to be dirty or to wear scuffed shoes. He makes his own bed and tidies up after himself."

"Can you describe the changes since the accident?"

A lump rose in my throat. I wiped my eyes with the back of my wrist. I told the doctor about Gideon's refusal to talk and the faraway place his mind goes during our lessons and his great fear of the carriage house.

"It sounds as if life with Gideon is both surprising and heartbreaking," said the doctor as he closed his notebook.

How well the doctor understood!

"Children like Gideon have a special claim on us," said the doctor. "In addition to that special claim, Gideon has suffered a deep trauma. You both have." He tapped his notebook thoughtfully with his pencil. "But I can help the both of you, if you're willing."

I grabbed his sleeve. "How?"

"Children like Gideon are born into all kinds of families, from the humblest cottage to even the greatest mansion. A child like Gideon weighs heavily upon family members who love them very much and want what's best for them."

Something inside shriveled. I shrank away from the doctor. "Gideon never weighed heavily on my parents! He doesn't weigh heavily on me!"

His eyes seemed to penetrate my brain so that he knew what I was thinking. "Are you being honest with yourself, Pringle? Don't you wish you could return to school? Continue your studies? See your friends again? Have you considered your future?" And then, he said, "Certainly, your mother and father considered your future, or they would not have sent you to boarding school."

Dr. van Lavender extracted a slim leaflet from his vest pocket. The leaflet had the same engraving as the letter that Uncle Edward had read in Father's library, so many weeks before. "I am the director of a school near Philadelphia," said the doctor. "It's a boarding school for children like Gideon."

"No!" I leaped to my feet. "Mother would never—"

The doctor smiled kindly. "Think of it this way. You attend boarding school for the best possible education, one that's suited to you, with your needs and interests at heart. Don't you want Gideon to have the same opportunity? One that's designed for children like him? One where there will be other children his age? Where he will study music and crafts and receive training in a trade? Doesn't he deserve that?" And then he added, "Don't you want a larger life for yourself? Don't you deserve that?"

I took the leaflet and turned over the doctor's words in my mind. My thoughts flew in every direction. I felt confused. I remembered the prayer I had prayed so long ago. I did want a larger life. The doctor offered the answer I'd yearned for.

A few nights later, Father's attorney, Mr. Royce, was our dinner guest. I always liked Mr. Royce and considered him a trusted family friend.

After the dishes were cleared, Uncle Edward called upon Ellen to sing.

My cousin has one of the clearest, prettiest

singing voices I've ever heard. I could see she loved the attention. Then she recited, "How Doth the Little Busy Bee" by Isaac Watts. My uncle's eyes glowed with pride.

"She belongs in the theater," said Mr. Royce.

Ellen's eyes shimmered at the praise. She clapped her hands together as if she couldn't believe that people were paid to sing and to dance and to show off.

"The theater is no place for our daughter," said Aunt Adeline.

Ellen's face burned with shame, the shimmer snuffed from her eyes.

In Ellen, I recognized a yearning so deep that I pitied her and envied her at the same time. I thought about how badly I wanted to return to Merrywood and a normal life. I understood what it's like to want something so badly it fills you up.

Right now I want sleep.

WEDNESDAY, SEPTEMBER 6, 1871

The last thing I heard last night was the conductor calling out Toledo, Ohio, at a quarter to midnight.

Around me, passengers are stirring. I've nudged Gideon awake so that he can take his turn at the toilet and wash basin.

Gideon snapped open his pocket watch. "Six thirty," he said.

The train has picked up speed, rushing us toward our new life. Outside, Lake Michigan glitters, stretching from horizon to horizon, as large as a sea.

I have one last story to tell, and then I'll close this diary and that part of my life. No more looking back! Only forward! In Chicago, everything will be different.

BEAUTIFUL DREAMER

It seems like a lifetime ago but it was just five days ago. Aunt Adeline had a terrible row with Uncle Edward over her allowance. My aunt thinks a woman of her station should have more money to spend.

The next day was a "Do Not Disturb Mama Day." We all stayed home from church and the curtains were drawn all day. We were relieved when Aunt Adeline took her afternoon tea in her room. Ellen sat in a chair, braiding the hair on a new doll, looking forlorn.

"Would you sing for me?" I asked.

Her eyes brightened and she scooted off the chair. "Want me to show you a dance?" She lifted the hem to her dress around her calves. "You won't tell Mama?"

I promised.

Ellen began to move her feet as she sang. *"Beautiful dreamer, wake unto me—"*

Upstairs, Aunt Adeline berated Mrs. Goodwin over something trivial. As her mother's voice rose, Ellen missed a step. She waited until her mother's tirade ended, and when the bedroom door slammed shut, she started over.

"Starlight and dewdrops are waiting for thee—"

As she sang, she clasped her hands together against her cheek. She bent at the knees and then arced both arms over her head and tiptoed in a circle.

I pulled Gideon from his chair. We copied Ellen's steps. It took several tries, but Gideon caught on. At last we had the steps and the words.

We sang and danced again, and when we finished, Ellen let go of our hands. She twirled on one foot, kicking out her leg as she turned. As she spun, she neared the table that held her mother's Rogers statue.

"Watch out!" I said.

Too late. Ellen kicked the table. The table wobbled and the statue sailed off. I dove toward the falling statue, but missed. It crashed to the floor and shattered. Clay pieces flew all over.

Horrified, Ellen leaped away.

"What was that?" shrieked Aunt Adeline. Her feet sounded like gunshots as she rushed down the stairs and into the parlor.

Aunt Adeline spotted the fragments, and then her eyes flew to the empty spot on the table. "Who did this?" she said, her eyes blue ice as she looked first to me and then to Gideon and then to Ellen. "Answer me."

"Mama," said Ellen as she raised her hand.

My legs quaked. I prepared to step between her

and her mother, to shield my cousin. I knew what her mother was capable of.

Ellen's raised hand turned into a pointing finger. "He did it, Mama. It's Gideon's fault."

Gideon stared blankly, not understanding.

Aunt Adeline's face contorted with fury. She slapped Gideon across the face, hard. She called him a terrible name and ordered him upstairs.

I glared at Ellen. "You lie!"

Ellen buried her face in her mother's dressing gown and sobbed.

"You've done nothing wrong, precious," said her mother.

I moved in front of Gideon. I didn't care what she did to me. I wasn't going to allow her to hurt my brother again.

At that moment, the front doorknob rattled. In walked Uncle Edward. He looked at Ellen clinging to her mother and sobbing. "What happened?"

Ellen sobbed louder and cleaved to her mother for protection. She knew I wanted to wring the truth from her!

"Oh, Edward," said Aunt Adeline, holding up a piece of the shattered statue. "Look what Gideon did."

Uncle Edward drew her to him. "I'll buy you another."

"Don't you see?" said Aunt Adeline. "It's not the statue. It's Gideon. He's not making any progress. No matter how hard I try. And now he's destructive. It's only a matter of time until he hurts someone. You've got to do something before Ellen gets hurt. If anything ever happened—"

Uncle Edward wiped Aunt Adeline's tears with his handkerchief, telling her, "I'll notify Dr. van Lavender first thing tomorrow morning."

KEEP ME FROM EVIL

That night, I wandered through Mother's room. I longed for a sense of Mother, but the scent of jasmine and violet had faded from the room, disappearing along with most of her things.

I sat at Mother's writing desk, a pretty desk with turned legs that Father had bought her from

France. I imagined her sitting there, writing letters to me. "What am I supposed to do, Mother?" I asked. "Shouldn't I be happy that Gideon will go to a special school? One for children like him?"

I opened the middle drawer of her desk. There lay Mother's Bible. Mother had a habit of copying her favorite verses in the front of her Bible. She had marked 1 Chronicles 4:10. It was Jabez's prayer.

"Oh, Mother," I cried. "Are you telling me that I deserve a larger life? Is that what you want for me? Weren't those your very words when I left for boarding school?"

The floorboards creaked. A hand touched on my shoulder. "Mother, I knew you would come!" I said, crying.

But it wasn't Mother. It was Mrs. Goodwin. I broke down in huge heaving sobs. "I miss my mother. I can't bear to feel this sad anymore."

"There, there," said Mrs. Goodwin, stroking my head. "You're grieving, dear. You're supposed to feel sad. It's something we do to heal."

She let me cry myself out, and then she said,

"Pringle, there's something I must tell you. You mustn't let them send Gideon away. It isn't right. He belongs with family."

"But Dr. van Lavender said—"

"What the doctor thinks and what he knows are two different things."

Mrs. Goodwin told me how her niece had a little girl just like Gideon. "The poor thing was two years old when her mother gave her up. When she died, no one could explain the black-and-blue marks on her little body."

"This school isn't that kind of place," I said.

"Maybe it is, maybe it isn't," said Mrs. Goodwin. "Are you willing to risk it? Can this doctor prove how many of his students turn out well in life?"

CHICAGO, ILLINOIS
1871

SATURDAY, SEPTEMBER 9, 1871

MOZIE AND MRS. DUGGAN

Four days have passed since the conductor called out La Porte, the last stop before Chicago, which meant we were less than sixty miles from our new life. The train was scheduled to arrive at nine twenty.

I remember staring out the window, mesmerized by the glittering lake, and thinking about how far we had traveled and hoping that Aunt Adeline and Uncle Edward and Ellen were sick with regret and worry.

Mozie had gobbled the last sausage and was washing himself. He is fastidious about his paws, ears, and whiskers.

"Do you think Aunt Adeline misses Mozie?" I asked Gideon.

Gideon doesn't understand sarcasm. He takes everything literally. "Mozie doesn't miss Aunt Adeline." He reached down to scratch Mozie's head. The cat grinned and stretched beneath Gideon's hand.

Aunt Adeline was happy to be rid of us, I was

sure. With us gone, she'd have more money to spend on her precious Rogers groups.

Gideon's and my money.

Someday, I vowed, I would return to Scranton and boot them out of my house and all the way to Kingdom Come.

I checked my carpetbag again. Miss Ringwald's letter was there, neatly folded. It felt comforting to think that my mother had once been a girl like me and that she and Miss Ringwald had gotten a switching after they climbed the bluff behind the chapel. What other mischief did they cause? Did she and Miss Ringwald hang upside down from the tree outside the library? Did they lie across their beds at night, sharing their diaries and letters and secrets?

I felt a pang of sadness. I missed Merricat terribly and longed to write to her. I missed Rabbit, too. Our departure happened so quickly. I had no time to leave him a note. What did he think? Was he worried? Was he hurt that I disappeared without a good-bye?

A squeal broke my gloom. It was Lucy, crawling on her hands and knees beneath the seats. Gwen was also on her hands and knees. She grabbed Lucy's foot and tried to pull her out, but Lucy's shoe came off in Gwen's hand.

"Lucy, come out this instant."

"I'm not Lucy. I'm a cat. Meow."

Lucy meowed again and crawled under the next seat, where the elder Mrs. Duggan was dozing.

Mrs. Duggan's eyes snapped open. "Mouse!" she screamed, slapping at her skirts and stamping her feet.

Up popped Lucy's head. "I'm not a mouse. I'm a cat." She meowed and licked Mrs. Duggan's hand.

"Oh, good gracious," said Mrs. Duggan, smoothing her skirts. "I declare, that child likes the feel of skin, doesn't she?" She excused herself and headed toward the toilet.

With Mrs. Duggan out of the way, Gwen latched on to Lucy's ankles. She dragged her out, feet first. Lucy's fingertips scraped along the floor.

Once in the aisle, Gwen lassoed her with both arms, but Lucy squirmed free and scooted under the next seat. She hissed and clawed the air.

"Come out here," said Gwen between clenched teeth. "Put your shoes on."

"Cats don't wear shoes," said Lucy.

Gwen reached the point where smoke was pouring out of her ears. She was at her wit's end, which explains what happened next. "You are not a cat," said Gwen. "You are a little girl named Lucy Pritchard who is going to get a spanking."

"Mother cats don't—" But Lucy couldn't finish that sentence. Gwen snatched Lucy, dragged her out again, turned her bottom side up, and gave her a good swatting.

Lucy howled.

Loud enough to make the forward car passengers think we had arrived at the Chicago station.

Loud enough to make the younger Mrs. Duggan and other prim-looking mothers and grandmothers smile with satisfaction as they pretended to look out the window.

In the midst of Lucy's howls, Gideon tapped me on the shoulder and whispered, "Mozie's gone." He pointed to the gaping carpetbag.

That explained the ear-piercing scream. The elder Mrs. Duggan found Mozie. He was using the toilet.

Even a cat likes his privacy in these matters. He swiped at Mrs. Duggan.

Mrs. Duggan fainted. That explained the thud.

The conductor pried opened the door. An indignant Mozie leaped over Mrs. Duggan and stalked haughtily back to our seat, where Gideon scooped him up.

A good dose of smelling salts brought Mrs. Duggan around. Aside from her scratched pride, she appeared in good health.

The conductor scolded us and said if we weren't so close to Chicago, he would toss Mozie off the train.

Gideon stuck out his chin and crossed his arms. "If Mozie goes, I go."

I told Gideon to hush, but the conductor's eyes were smiling even if his mouth was not.

OUR HORROR

Little did I know that our train was running late.

Little did I know that our engineer had stoked the engine and was making up lost time.

Little did I know we were barreling toward disaster at a full thirty-five miles per hour.

After washing the children's faces, combing their hair, and fastening their shoes, Gwen looked affright. I offered to mind the children so she could primp for her husband.

Gwen got out her brush and comb and hairpins and headed into the washroom. I gathered the children around me and began to teach them a game Merricat and I played called "Throwing the Smile." Lucy beat us all. She set her mouth and squinched her eyes and managed not to smile or giggle, no matter how many smiles we threw at her.

Just as it was Adam's turn, Mozie clawed his way out of the carpetbag, leaped over our laps, and streaked into the men's compartment.

"Crazy cat," I said.

Little did I know that Mozie was the smartest

one of us all. The floor trembled. A few seconds later, it shuddered.

A shudder is never a good thing. In Scranton, if the ground trembles, it means something terrible has happened at the mines – a cave-in or an explosion. Every miner knows if the rats head up the slope, drop your tools and get out.

"Stay down," I said, pushing the children to the floor. "Cover your heads." For once they listened to me, and just as they put their arms over their heads, our carriage pitched sideways.

The screams! The car tilted one direction and then the other, tossing us like rag dolls across the aisle and back again. Overhead, the lanterns swung wildly. The car creaked and groaned and leaned precariously to one side. For a second, we hovered there, and then, with a great creak and moan and splintering of wood and glass, the car toppled over onto its side. We were flung against the carriage wall. With my shoulder, I shielded Sallie from the brunt of the force.

Then all was still. In the distance, iron wheels screeched against iron rails. As if an alarm sounded, we all moved at once, turning into a jumble of arms and legs and bodies, clambering for the windows and doors, now overhead.

Hands reached into our wrecked car. The children clung to me and cried for their mother. I passed Sallie through the window into a stranger's arms. How she wailed! Next went Lucy – kicking and crying for me – and then Adam and then Gideon and me.

Outside, Lucy looked around wildly and began to cry, "Mama!"

I gaped at the cars. Our car and two others lay completely on their sides, each a distance from the other, each splintered wood.

I turned into someone who gave orders. "You must listen to me. You are in my army and I am your captain."

I grabbed Lucy's hand and stuck it inside Gideon's right hand and said, "Hold Lucy's hand. Do not let go. That's an order."

I grabbed Adam's hand and stuck him to Gideon's left hand. "Stay together. That's another order."

The younger Mrs. Duggan was walking in a circle, looking dazed and calling for Mother Duggan. Her forehead was cut and bleeding. I peeled Sallie from my hip, handed her to Mrs. Duggan, and told her, "Mind the baby."

Numbly, she took Sallie.

Sallie's lower lip stuck out and she screwed up her little face and bawled. It hurt to ignore her reaching arms, but I picked up my skirts and dashed back to the car.

Several men scrambled over the sides of the cars, helping to extricate passengers. The cars looked like giant insects with waving arms and legs and heads of passengers climbing out of the windows, not caring whose head or shoulders they used as a footstool.

On the ground, men and women were lying about, groaning. Others sat, holding handkerchiefs to their faces. Some were weeping. In a mixture of foreign words and accents, forward-car passengers tended the hurt and the dazed, wiping their faces, giving them water.

"Gwen!" I called.

A dark fear rooted itself in my stomach. Was she still inside the washroom? Was she injured? Unable to climb out? Or worse? Just as the fear numbed my legs and arms, I heard my name. "Pringle!"

Just as the fear spread to my arms and legs, Gwen emerged through a window. A man lifted her and helped her down. She stumbled toward me, her hair sailing about her shoulders and her dress dirty and torn. She cradled her right arm. "My children! Where are my children?"

I steadied her. "Yes, everyone's safe." I led her to Gideon, standing like a soldier, clutching Lucy's and Adam's hands. Sallie leaped toward Gwen and dug her knees into Gwen's waist and held on for dear life.

Gwen dropped to her knees and covered her children with kisses, as any mother would.

Mrs. Duggan rushed off to find the elder Mrs. Duggan, and I found a doctor, a German man who examined Gwen's right arm and pronounced her elbow broken. He wrapped and splinted her arm and said it would mend in six weeks. I translated for Gwen, and he complimented me on my German.

"You speak German?" said Gwen.

"Ein wenig," I said.

"Anything else?" said Gwen.

"Un peu de la langue française."

"You are full of surprises, Pringle."

Soon, farmers arrived with teams of horses to clear the wrecked cars. Their wives came, too, bringing baskets of food and jugs of water and bandages.

Another German passenger took it upon himself to examine the wrecked cars. In a heavy accent, he shouted that the axle in the last car was defective.

The defective axle had caused the last car to derail, he explained, and when it derailed, it pulled the second and third cars from the track. Each car was dragged about three hundred feet before it broke loose and toppled over.

A woman remarked that we were fortunate the car's coal stove and lanterns weren't lit, or they would have set the wooden carriage on fire, just like the Angola tragedy four years ago in western New York. Forty-nine people were crushed or burned to death when the last two cars jumped the track and tumbled into an icy gorge.

What an uproar that caused! The men passengers banded together and insisted that the German man inspect the still-standing cars.

Together, the German man and the engineer climbed over and around and beneath each car. After a lengthy inspection, they declared the remaining twelve cars safe for travel. Other men passengers rescued our carpetbags and personal belongings.

We piled into the second-class cars, crowded and weary and shaken but grateful that no one had died.

As the gratefulness wore off, some passengers got to talking. They blamed the engineer for stoking the engine. Others blamed the railroad company for the defective axle. Others deemed it an accident and an accident can't be helped. They said accidents are God's will.

God's will, my thumb! God doesn't will a rear

axle to bend and disengage. God doesn't will a train engineer to speed up and a railroad car to jump a track any more than God wills a carriage carrying a mother and a father to tumble down a ravine.

The two Mrs. Duggans were reunited, and the older Mrs. Duggan was unharmed, except for a bump on her head and bruises on her paper-thin skin. Gwen huddled her children like a mother hen brooding her chicks. Lucy clung to her mother and kept her shoes on all the way to Chicago.

Our only loss was Mozie. We called and called, but our dear cat was nowhere to be found. I am sick about it and tried not to cry when we had to board without him.

Gideon disappeared inside himself. I squeezed his hand and told him that it was all right and to come back when he was ready. Before you get over a loss, you must move through the loss.

After a while, Gideon leaned his head on my shoulder and two tears trailed down his cheeks. He wiped his face with his handkerchief and whispered, "Mozie's a good hunter," and I said, "A capital killer."

That's when I knew Gideon would be all right. Together we prayed for Mozie to have a good long hunting life on the shores of Lake Michigan.

It's nearly midnight. My eyes feel gritty. My hand is sore from writing. Tomorrow I'll write about our grand welcome at Miss Ringwald's.

SUNDAY, SEPTEMBER 10, 1871

SAYING GOOD-BYE TO THE PRITCHARDS

At long last, the train reached Chicago and continued slowly northward through the city. "She-caw-go! She-caw-go!" the conductor shouted. A thrill ran up my spine.

The train whistle sounded as we approached the LaSalle station. The train rumbled across a series of switches. Its brakes squealed and it ground to a halt. The boilers hissed and exhaled. Their great breath drifted past the train windows.

The conductor rushed to set the steps in place. My face felt pulled down as passengers scanned the crowd for loved ones. Gideon and I had no one to welcome us, and now we had to bid good-bye to

Gwen and her little ones. I felt homesick for the Pritchards already.

How is it that you can know someone for only three days and yet feel as though you've known them a lifetime? Some might say that near tragedy brought us closer, but that's not the reason, or else I would feel just as close to the Duggans.

Mother said this happens when our spirit connects with another person's spirit. Perhaps the two spirits recognize one another from a different time and place.

As I waited for the doors to open, a deep sadness coursed through me, sweeping me down a river I didn't want to sail. I swallowed hard and lifted Sallie onto my hip and clutched Lucy's hand.

Gwen's feet had barely touched the platform when a man with red hair and stylish goatee and wearing a tailored frock coat and narrow tie pushed through the crowd, calling, "Gwen! Gwen!"

"Papa!" Lucy and Adam sang out and threw themselves at his legs.

Sallie whipped her little head around and tried to leap out of my arms.

Did Mr. Peter Pritchard care that Gwen stood in the middle of a crowded platform? That women wearing fancy dresses and hats twittered like scolding birds?

"Avert your eyes," he told the children.

Lucy and Adam giggled and covered their eyes but peeked through outspread fingers as their father scooped up their mother and whirled her around twice. Her dress sailed out like a bell and he kissed her the whole while in a way that made me blush and grow warm inside and think about Rabbit.

Forcing the corners of my mouth up, I knelt by Adam and Lucy. "Now, you must help your mother and take good care of her. You only get one mother."

Gwen's eyes were bright with sorrow. "I'm going to miss you, Pringle. How would I have managed without you? Promise you'll visit." With her good hand, she unclasped her little purse and took out a plain yellow calling card and pressed it into my hand. It gave her address on Sherman Street.

Scowling fiercely, Lucy crossed her arms. "I don't want Pringle to go."

Adam hopped up and down like a rabbit. "Please please please visit us," he said. "Gideon's my friend. I want to play with Gideon."

I choked up, hearing that, and bit my lip so I wouldn't cry. Gideon's first true friend!

Mrs. Duggan and Mrs. Duggan strolled toward us, accompanied by a skinny, pimple-faced young man whom I presumed to be the infamous Duggan heir. His waistcoat and trousers flapped around him, making him look like laundry that had run away from a clothesline.

"Oh, Mrs. Pritchard!" trilled the younger Mrs. Duggan. "This is my son, Harold. Did I tell you he's a student at Harvard University?"

"At the top of his class, just like his father," piped the elder Mrs. Duggan. With a grand flourish, she offered her calling card. "If you wish to call, here's our address on Pine Street."

Pine Street! Well, that's the street where Miss Ringwald lives, and I was about to tell her that we'd soon be neighbors, but Mr. Pritchard asked Harold Duggan how he was doing in his classes and if Professor Brown still pulled out his glass eye and polished it on his sleeve.

Harold laughed. "At the beginning of every semester, and at parties, to shock the ladies."

Mr. Pritchard guffawed and slapped his leg and said Mr. Brown hasn't changed one bit and to give him Peter Pritchard's best regards. "Our families go back a long ways. Why, when Robert Lincoln and I—"

The eyes on the Mrs. Duggans popped at the mention of our late President's son. "You know Robert Lincoln?" asked the younger Mrs. Duggan.

"We were classmates for a short time at Harvard, before I joined the Union Army," said Mr. Pritchard. "His father was a great man."

The Duggans stood there, trying to make sense out of Peter Pritchard, who attended Harvard and who knew Robert Lincoln and his father. Their eyes ran all over Mr. Pritchard, and then over Gwen, from top to bottom, and suddenly she didn't seem so common. Gwen smiled politely at them.

Just before they left, the younger Mrs. Duggan sidled up to Gwen and said, "It would be lovely to have you for tea, Mrs. Pritchard."

A slight should always be ignored, and that's just what Gwen did, which showed impeccably good manners. Gwen tucked Mrs. Duggan's calling card in her purse. "I'll look forward to that visit. Thank you for putting up with my little ones."

"Oh, those dear, sweet children! Speak nothing of it," said Mrs. Duggan, patting Lucy on the head.

Lucy grinned like the Cheshire cat.

The Pritchards departed in one direction, and Gideon and I headed for the cab rank. It was early evening, and the sun was setting in a scarlet haze over the prairie west of the city. A steady, stiff wind whipped at my skirts.

Chicago has over 330,000 people, and we passed every single one. Its busyness swept my breath away. The streets teemed with pedestrians—tourists, farmers, immigrants, workingmen, businessmen in frock coats—and horse cars and buggies and carriages, all hurrying to get someplace else.

I found the cab rank and stepped up to the first hack. I winced at its sorry-looking horse with its sway back and bandaged forelegs. I gave the driver Miss Ringwald's name and address.

The driver curled his lip. "Ringwald! That crazy woman who runs around spouting nonsense about animals as if they were people! If she read her Bible, she'd know God gave man dominion over the animals and the earth." He went on to say several nasty things about Miss Ringwald.

Such arrogance! Beatrice Ringwald is a passionate, well-educated woman. She holds strong opinions on religion and politics. She's unconventional, but she's not crazy, and she's not any of the other things he called her.

"Where do you preach?" I asked.

He seemed pleased at my mistake. "I'm no preacher," he said.

"Good," I said. "I'm paying for a cab ride, not a sermon."

The driver dropped his jaw so wide his rotting molars showed. He snapped his mouth shut so quickly his teeth clicked. "You ain't paying for no cab ride," he sneered. "Have a nice walk."

He flapped the reins and the cab started down the street without us. His poor horse walked tenderly. "Your horse needs shoes!" I shouted after him. "Dominion means to take better care of your horse." I wished I could have performed a citizen's arrest.

Along came another hack. This time I provided a neighboring address. The cabbie whistled. "Swanky neighborhood."

As the horse bobbed along, the cabbie explained how the city's downtown was centered on the mouth of the Chicago River. The river's two branches divided the city into the West, South, and North divisions. The wealthy live along the lakeshore and parts of the north side, he explained. The poor live in neighborhoods to the south and west of the downtown.

"Everywhere you look, we're sprouting new buildings and more houses," he said, gesturing grandly. He called Chicago the biggest boomtown the world has ever seen. "It's the hub for nearly every railroad," he said. "Thousands of people funnel through its depots every day, just like you."

He went on to describe how, every day, trains full of timber arrive from Wisconsin for all the new construction. Every day, cattle and hogs arrive for slaughter, because Chicago is the meatpacking center of America. Every day, corn, wheat, and barley pour in from the plains, because Chicago is the world's largest grain port.

The cab continued north, past tall three-story commercial buildings. The most prominent building was the courthouse, with its gleaming white limestone façade. The evening sun gleamed yellow off its tall dome that rose above the surrounding buildings.

"See that dome?" said the cabbie. "Inside hangs

the largest bronze bell you've ever seen. Over eleven thousand pounds! And loud! You can hear it all over the city. That bell tells you when to rise, when to eat your dinner, and when to quit work."

Just then, the huge bell began to toll. Gideon clapped his hands over his ears. The cabbie shouted over the din. "That bell also tells you when there's a fire. We've got lookouts posted on the courthouse balcony. At the first sign of smoke, they sound the alarm. But that's not all. We've also got one hundred and seventy-two alarm boxes, situated at key points all over the city."

A clanging fire truck grew closer. Gideon gripped the sides of the cab as a hose truck clattered down a cross street.

"And we've got the most professional firefighters in these United States," said the cabbie. "We've got seventeen steam engines, four hook-and-ladder trucks, two hose elevators, and one hundred and eighty-five paid firefighters. Paid firemen! Now that's a newfangled idea."

The cabbie grew gloomy. "The only trouble, if

you ask me, but of course no one ever does, is all this wood. Everything's made out of wood because wood goes up so quickly and it's cheap. You never saw so many cheap houses that a good wind could blow away. Why, even our streets and sidewalks are pinewood. One spark in the right place, and *whoosh!*" The cabbie snapped his fingers. "The entire city could go up in flames. If you ask me, but nobody ever does, we're sitting in a tinderbox."

We crossed the North Branch of the Chicago River. Soon the cabbie turned onto Pine Street. Swanky, the cabbie had called it, and he was right. The houses grew steadily larger, even larger than the grandest houses in Scranton. At first they occupied half a city block, but within a short distance, the houses swelled to take up an entire block. The streets were lined with magnificent trees and beautiful gardens.

At a gabled mansion, the driver slowed the horse and turned into the long, curving driveway.

"You're lucky," he said, nodding toward Gideon. "Not many employers would hire someone with—"

He wasn't an unkind man, and so I overlooked his pitying look. "We have a special situation," I said.

We jumped out, grabbed our carpetbags, and started toward the front door. The driver motioned for me to go around back to the servant's entrance.

I gave him a small wave. He tapped his hat "good-bye" and started down the drive.

Once the carriage rounded the corner, I grabbed Gideon's hand and pulled him down the driveway and across the street toward the next block, where the house number matched Miss Ringwald's.

And what a house! It was a massive three-story stone house with matching towers at each corner and a mansard roof with ten windows.

The wide front door was intricately carved with swirls, reminding me of Miss Ringwald's own flamboyant nature. I finger-combed Gideon's hair in place. "Tuck in your shirttails," I told him.

I twisted the knob on the large brass doorbell. It made a loud metallic burring sound. Oh! The tintinnabulation from my knees knees knees! How they knocked with excitement!

THE FISH FOOTMAN

After several knee-knocking minutes, a tall, slim, waxy-faced manservant answered the door. With bulging eyes, he scrutinized us from head to toe and then stared over our heads stupidly at the sky. "Those seeking employment must use the rear entrance." He swung the door shut.

"I'm not seeking employment!" I yelled at the door and pushed against it.

"Now see here, miss," said the manservant. He pushed back. The door closed with a slam. It felt like a slap.

I dug out Miss Ringwald's letter and twisted the bell again.

It took several twists before the manservant returned. Again he stared stupidly at the sky and said, "Those seeking charity—"

"Charity! I'm not seeking charity. My name is Miss Pringle Rose and I'm calling on Miss Ringwald."

He shot out a white-gloved hand. It held a silver tray. "Your card?"

I had no calling card. Instead, I dropped the letter in the tray.

He stared, unblinking, at the envelope. He sniffed and stepped back, pulling the door wider for us to pass through. "Very well, miss. You may wait here."

He stalked off.

"Fish or frog footman?" I whispered to Gideon.

"Fish footman," said Gideon.

"Pickerel or trout?"

"Trout," said Gideon.

It felt as though we had landed in Wonderland. Crystal pendants dangled from an enormous chandelier. The pendants scattered brilliant, dizzying sunlight on the walls, foyer table, and black-and-white marble floor. The foyer felt as though it were turning.

It's not polite to speak of other people's money, let alone count it, but everything about the foyer, from its marbled floor to its sweeping marble staircase spoke not just of wealth, but vast wealth.

I squeezed Gideon's hand. I couldn't help but think how comfortable Gideon and I would be here and how grateful I felt to Beatrice Ringwald for her willingness to help us.

Shoes clicked down the hall. A tall, gray-haired figure strode forward. "You know my daughter?"

I had seen fathers like Mr. Ringwald at Merrywood. They were the sort of men who entered a room chin first. "My mother, Eliza Duncan, and Miss Ringwald were classmates at Merrywood School for Girls."

From the silver tray, he picked up the letter. "May I?" he asked, and I nodded. He opened the letter and flicked his eyes over its words. "This letter was written over four months ago."

He returned the letter to its envelope and handed it to me without a word about my parents. It was rude of him. "I'm sorry to disappoint you," said Mr. Ringwald. "My daughter no longer lives here."

I must have blinked a hundred times. "Pardon?"

Her father said, "My daughter is under a doctor's care at Bellevue Place."

"Is she ill?"

"It's a private sanitarium."

I gasped. "Sanitarium! You mean a mental asylum?"

Her father ignored my question. "Surely you have family in Chicago. Surely you would not have traveled such a distance alone."

There was that falling feeling again, the feeling that I was spiraling down a deep, dark hole. We had come so far. We could not return home.

Gideon tugged on my sleeve and whispered, "Adam."

The falling feeling stopped as I remembered Gwen's calling card. "Of course, we have someplace to go."

"It's settled, then," said Mr. Ringwald. "I'll have my driver bring the carriage around."

That's how I found myself sobbing in the Pritchards' parlor, where Gwen pulled me into a tight embrace and patted my back, saying, "There, there," over and over again.

Why do those two words soothe so much?

In the children's room, Gwen made up a bed for Gideon and me—just a nest of quilts and bedspreads, really—but I slept through the night for the first time in months.

MONDAY, SEPTEMBER 11, 1871

The Pritchards live in a cramped but tasteful two-story frame house on Sherman Street on the South Side of Chicago. The parlor carpet was once fine, judging by its colors and pattern, but is worn thin. The furniture is sturdy but spare. There's not one framed photograph or ornamental plate or knick-knack or Rogers group statue.

Peter works as an organizer for the National Labor Union. He publishes a small, single-sheet labor newspaper, which he started with a small inheritance from his father. (Oh, what would Father say to that! Never mind. I know.)

This morning we breakfasted on tea and toast

and baked beans, dark with molasses. I sat Gideon down for his morning lessons, and Adam and Lucy joined in.

Lucy has a quick mind. She's just four but she recognizes upper- and lowercase letters and can sound out simple words.

After lessons, I read to the children, just as Mother did for Gideon and me so that we would learn to read dramatically and with great feeling. I read "A Mad Tea Party" from *Alice's Adventures in Wonderland*, using different voices for the different characters, the way Mother always did. That made the children laugh.

A sad look came to Gwen's eyes and I could tell she was someplace far away. I let her visit there and continued reading to the children.

TUESDAY, SEPTEMBER 12, 1871

A barn caught fire on LaSalle Street and we could see the plumes of smoke. The minute my back was turned, Gideon and Adam sneaked away from morning lessons to follow the clanging wagons.

They stayed away a very long time. "It's what

boys do," said Gwen. I suppose she is right, for the streets are filled with boys playing marbles and chasing each other. I am happy that Gideon has found a true friend.

Summer should have ended, but Chicago is hot and sticky and dirty. Peter blames it on the wind, which blows from the southwest, bringing in waves of heat from the prairie.

The trees droop from a lack of rain. The grass and leaves are crisp and dry and lie in heaps against the houses. Everything appears an odd, washed-out brown, like a sepia photograph. Even the horses look exhausted as they clop down the streets. I feel sorry for the horses that pull the fire equipment and sorrier for the firemen, who are bleary-eyed with exhaustion because they're on call twenty-four hours a day.

LATER

Peter brought home a copy of the *Chicago Tribune*. I paged through the newspaper, looking over the advertisements, hoping to find employment.

Here are the jobs I found:

WANTED—A GIRL TO WASH bottles, and fill them up, at No. 16 Franklin-st., basement, at 9 o'clock.

WANTED—A GOOD SMART girl to cook. Apply at 99 North Wells-st.

WANTED—LAUNDRY GIRL AT restaurant. 77 Dearborn-st.

WANTED—A GOOD CHAMBERmaid, one that can wait on table. Apply before 10 a.m. at 124 South State-st.

The sad truth is that I have no skills. Someone else has always washed my dishes, cooked my meals, polished my furniture, stitched and sewed and ironed and washed my clothes. But this advertisement looks promising:

WANTED—A YOUNG GIRL 12 to 15 years of age to assist in the care of a child. HOWARD HOUSE, corner State and Van Buren.

I have asked Peter and Gwen for a letter of reference. Peter promised to think it over and give me an answer in the morning.

A hot, sticky breeze is blowing through the window. I have bundled up Mother's cape for a pillow. I can hear Peter's and Gwen's murmurs. They're probably listing all the reasons they cannot provide me with a reference: I have no skills. I have no true work experience. Gwen has only known me for ten days. They do not know my background.

My great-great-grandmother Annabella came to America at fourteen, with only a silver needle and thimble and this scarlet cape, but her spinning and weaving and sewing skills allowed her to make her way in a new country.

I feel stupid and useless. What good did my studies at Merrywood do?

WEDNESDAY, SEPTEMBER 13, 1871

At breakfast, Peter tapped his teacup with a butter knife. "Children, I have an announcement."

Gwen cleared her throat and corrected Peter, saying, "We."

"*We* have an announcement," said Peter. "If Pringle is willing, we'd like her to stay on as your nursemaid."

Gwen lifted her splinted arm. "Heaven knows, I need a nursemaid."

Adam and Lucy shouted, "Yes!" Sallie banged her cup.

And so the Pritchards have taken pity on Gideon and me. In exchange for room and board, I will work as a nursemaid for Adam, Lucy, and Sallie.

Imagine that! Pringle Rose, a nursemaid. Perhaps I'll stay until I'm somebody else.

LATER

I have never done the marketing before, but today I bought a cabbage, onions, carrots, turnips, and a shinbone of beef. I wasn't sure how to select the best vegetables, and so I watched another woman pick and choose, her fingers expertly squeezing this one and thumping that one.

The huckster was a pleasant man. I marveled at the pinewood streets and sidewalks, and he told me that wood is treated to look like stone and brick. I thought of all the good that wooden streets and sidewalks would do for ladies' dresses and shoes, especially on rainy days.

"Chicago is famous for its muddy streets," said the huckster. "Why, one time I passed a gentleman up to his waist in mud. I offered to help him, but he said, 'No, thanks. I've got a fine horse beneath me.'"

THURSDAY, SEPTEMBER 14, 1871

"If you can read, you can cook." That's Gwen's motto. She handed me *Mrs. Goodfellow's Cookery As It Should Be*, and I followed the instructions and made soup.

First I cut the beef into chunks and laid it in the bottom of a heavy pot with a lump of butter. Then I cut up some herbs and laid them over the beef. I covered the pot tightly and set it over a low fire.

When the gravy was almost dried up, I filled the pot with water and let it boil. I spooned the fat and scum from the top into a jar that Gwen saves for soap fat. Then I grated five turnips, three carrots, and half of a cabbage and now it's simmering a good long while and smells delicious.

LATER

Peter ate three bowls of soup.

In between spoonfuls, Peter talked about the American workers' fight for an eight-hour workday. "Imagine eight hours for work, eight to do as you will, and eight to rest," said Peter. "Some day every worker will have an eight-hour workday, and he will thank a union."

Father called unions a dangerous plot. Father said unions are un-American, because they go against our capitalist economy because they interfere with the rights of industrialists and private individuals.

"Should a worker dictate to his employer how

he should manage his shop?" I asked Peter. "A shop in which the employer has invested his own capital?"

"A worker has invested his capital, too," said Peter. "A worker's capital is his legs and arms and back. Why shouldn't he negotiate his worth?"

"If a worker doesn't like his employer's terms, then he should go elsewhere to work," I said. "For example, the striking coal workers are foreign-born. They forget that we invited them to our shores to be good workers. Perhaps they should remember that they earn more in America and enjoy more freedoms – including the freedom to work where they want – than in their homelands."

"That's true," said Peter. "But should we expect our workers to leave their customs and habits and convictions and principles behind? Why are we surprised when they bring their desire for better working conditions here to America?"

Peter scowled and grew quiet. *Oh, dear,* I thought, as his scowl deepened. Did I make Peter angry? Did I say too much? At home, Father would have enjoyed such a discussion. He liked to hear my opinions. "Would you like to debate or discuss?" That's what Father would say. If I chose *debate*, he would happily take the opposing side, just for fun.

Suddenly, Peter slapped the table and jumped up. "Pringle!" he shouted. "Thank you! You have given me an idea for my editorial!" He grabbed his coat and hat and headed back to his office.

FRIDAY, SEPTEMBER 15, 1871

This morning, Peter said, "Gideon, how would you like to work for me?"

"How much?" said Gideon.

Peter said fifteen cents.

Gideon said fifty cents.

"Gideon!" I said. "Mind your manners!"

But Peter said, "Every worker deserves the right to negotiate honest wages for an honest day's work."

To Gideon, he said, "Twenty-five cents," and Gideon said, "Yes," and Peter said, "You drive a hard bargain." He held out his hand for Gideon to shake.

We've only spent one week with the Pritchards, and my brother has converted from Capitalist to Proletariat.

LATER

It's nearly a straight walk to Peter's office. Gideon walked with great purpose, swinging his arms and whistling.

"Look at his self-importance," said Peter. "That's what honest work and fair wages do for a man."

We passed the South Side Gas Works and the Armory and Police Court and then turned onto Madison. Peter's office building sits just three blocks from the Courthouse. The building is three stories tall. As we clomped up the dark stairway, I could hear the offices humming with activity.

Peter has rented two rooms on the third floor. On the door facing the landing, the words LABOR'S LAMP glowed in gilt lettering on frosted glass.

Peter puffed with pride as he turned the key. The front room was stuffy and crammed with furniture, papers, and books. Two desks were stacked with papers and books. Still more papers and books cluttered bookcases and tables. The waste cans overflowed with crumpled papers.

"You know what they say," said Peter. "A cluttered desk is a sign of a cluttered mind."

"It's better than an empty desk," I said.

Peter laughed. "You're a very smart girl."

He lifted the window. A breeze passed through, fluttering scraps of paper hanging from nails driven into the wall behind Peter's desk. Naggers, Peter called them, because each scrap nagged him about something important, a quotation he liked, an idea for an editorial, or an overdue bill to pay.

Peter led us to the small back room, taken up by a tall iron printing press. "The big newspapers use steam-operated presses," said Peter. "Here, we print by hand."

To Gideon, he said, "Can you count to one hundred?"

"Easy," said Gideon.

"Good," said Peter. "After we print the run, you'll count out one hundred newspapers and tie them with string for the newsboys to hawk."

Peter showed Gideon the closet where the broom, dustpan, bucket, and mop were kept. "Your job is to sweep the floors, empty the trash, and tidy the office," said Peter.

Gideon was beside himself with joy. To think he was getting paid to count and sweep!

Just as I turned to leave, Peter wrote something on a scrap of paper and poked it through a nail. "God helps those who can't help themselves," it said.

My hand flew to my heart. Those were Miss Ringwald's very words.

SATURDAY, SEPTEMBER 16, 1871

Hot! These days dry a person out! And still no sign of rain.

The courthouse bell tolled and fire trucks thundered past us as Gideon and I headed to Peter's office. Smoke curled up from a west-side neighborhood across the river.

Gideon begged to follow the firemen, but I said no, that he's a worker now and that he has a job to do. Angry! He stomped all the way to Peter's office.

Later, three more fires broke out on Canal, Washington, and Franklin streets. Peter took Gideon to see the Franklin Street fire. With glowing eyes, Gideon told us how the firemen ran around, shouting orders and hosing down the fire with streams of water, and how the hoses turned the streets to mud.

"When I grow up, I want to be a fireman," he said, and Peter said, "That's good. Chicago needs all the firemen it can get."

Peter said the city had 669 fires last year. 669! That made Gideon worry that there wouldn't be any fires left for him when he's old enough to be a fireman.

SUNDAY, SEPTEMBER 17, 1871

This evening Gideon and I attended services with Gwen and Peter and the children at the Methodist Church on Clark Street. The minister gave a lovely sermon that exercised my mind. The hymns exercised my lungs and vocal cords.

Methodists, it seems, are determined to show

they can sing louder and faster and with more courage than anyone else. But the tunes are catchy and now "Love Divine, All Loves Excelling" keeps running through my head.

Imagine that! Pringle Rose, a Methodist!

MONDAY, SEPTEMBER 18, 1871

A terrible tragedy has befallen a poor family not far from Peter's office. Yesterday, a mother locked her two young children, ages five and three, in the kitchen while she attended morning church services.

A policeman spotted smoke coming from the house and turned in the fire alarm. The neighbors heard the children's cries, but by the time they broke down the door, the children had died from smoke inhalation.

The newspaper says the mother is crazy with grief. She is a widow and has no family. Why would a mother leave her children alone?

TUESDAY, SEPTEMBER 19, 1871

So intently was Peter looking over large sheets of the *Labor's Lamp* with his assistant, an older colored man named Mr. Wallace, that the two men didn't notice Gideon and me.

"The proofs look good," said Peter to Mr. Wallace. "Go on home."

Mr. Wallace shook his head. "I'll stay until you're finished."

"I'm working late," said Peter, moving papers and books to clear a space on his desk. "I don't need a nursemaid."

"You got another letter today."

Peter waved off Mr. Wallace's words. "It proves nothing except that someone is reading our little newspaper."

"This one's uglier than the others, Peter."

Peter pulled out his chair sharply, sat, and mulled over papers on his desk. Without looking up, he shooed the older man away. "Go home or I'll fire you."

Mr. Wallace laughed. "You can't fire me, Peter. You know I hid the key to the toilet room."

"That key is the only reason I haven't fired you."

"I know," piped Gideon.

The two men noticed us for the first time. Mr. Wallace held one finger to his lips. "Shhh."

Gideon buttoned his lip.

Mr. Wallace pulled his cap over his head. "You are too headstrong for your own good, Peter Pritchard." Mr. Wallace closed the door behind him. His footsteps creaked down the hall and down the stairs.

Peter's eyes met mine. "How much of that did you hear?"

"Everything," I said, eyeing the letters on his desk.

Peter stuck the letters in his desk drawer. "Mr. Wallace doesn't know the difference between a threat and an opinion," he said, but I know Peter was lying to me.

WEDNESDAY, SEPTEMBER 20, 1871

HOW TO MAKE BLACK PUDDING

Take three quarts of sheep's blood. Add one spoonful of salt. Boil a quart of fine hominy in enough water to let the hominy swell.

While the hominy is cooking, pound nutmeg, mace, cloves, and allspice. Cut one pound of hog's fat into small bits. Add parsley, sage, sweet herbs, and one pint of bread crumbs. Add one pound of hog's fat. Mix well. Add the hominy and blood and mix well again.

Stuff this mixture into cleaned pork skins from intestine. Tie links. Prick skins so that the sausages don't burst. Boil twenty minutes. Cover the puddings with clean straw until they're cold.

FRIDAY, SEPTEMBER 22, 1871

Day after day, it's the patter of little feet. Some days I feel as though I'm being ordered around by mice and rabbits. I feel like Alice growing taller and then smaller, struggling to find her right size. It's a curious sort of life, but the busyness helps with the sadness I sometimes feel.

The key to managing three small children is a system. Here is our daily routine: In the morning, I dress the children, make them tea and toast and boiled egg or porridge, make them eat tea and toast and boiled egg or porridge, make them clean up after themselves, and make them do their morning lessons.

All this while, I am flying from the table to the cookstove, where I'm fixing the midday meal, soup or stew or potatoes in their jackets. I make them eat (again!), make them clean up after themselves (again!), and then it's afternoon naps for Lucy and Sallie.

I hate to see Sallie cry when I put her to bed. Her little lip sticks out and pure betrayal crosses her face. She sobs inconsolably for five minutes and then plops herself facedown and falls asleep. While Sallie naps, I walk Gideon to work, and then come straight home and run around, tidying the house and making the evening meal.

At seven, it's growing dark and I am tired to the bone. Peter and Gideon walk home together.

All through supper, Gideon talks a blue streak about work. He is so full of self-importance that you'd think he owns the newspaper!

Then it's time to clear the dishes and wash the dishes and ready the children for bed and read to Adam, Lucy, and Gideon.

After that, my head is so thick with tiredness that I collapse on the bedding in the corner of the room that I share with the children. This morning, Gideon told me I snore.

SATURDAY, SEPTEMBER 23, 1871

Gideon found a mother cat and four kittens in an alley near Peter's office building. The kittens' eyes are opened, and that means they're at least ten days old. Peter says the cat and her kittens can stay, but Gideon will have to find homes for the kittens as soon as they're old enough to leave their mother. Gideon made them a comfortable bed out of rags in the broom closet.

SUNDAY, SEPTEMBER 24, 1871

True to their spiritual nature, Adam and Gideon slept through this evening's sermon, but as soon as the benediction was given, they turned as awake as owls and chased each other home.

The nights are so hot that that the air feels like a hand pressing down on me, and each time I breathe, I am gulping hot air. Through the open window, I can hear the distant ringing of the courthouse bell and the clang of the fire trucks, but I do little more than roll over and fall back to sleep. I told this to Gwen and she said, "Pringle, you are a true Chicagoan."

MONDAY, SEPTEMBER 25, 1871

TOO AND TWO

Tonight Peter wriggled his eyebrows and said, "Why should the number two hundred and eighty-eight never be mentioned in mixed company?"

Gwen grew alarmed. "Peter! The children!"

Peter said, "You're right. The answer is too gross."

Gwen flapped her napkin at Peter, pretending to be annoyed, but I could tell she was trying not to laugh.

"What does 'too gross' mean?" asked Adam.

Peter and Gwen were too busy giggling to hear, and so Adam asked me, "What does 'too gross' mean?"

"If you have twelve eggs, how many eggs do you have?" I said.

"One dozen," said Adam.

"If you have twelve dozen eggs, you have one hundred and forty-four eggs. One hundred and forty-four is one gross. So two gross are twenty-four dozen, or two hundred and eighty-eight eggs."

"What's so funny about that?" said Lucy. "I can't count that high."

"I can," said Gideon, and he started to count. "1–2–3–"

I tried to discourage him, but Peter said, "No, let's hear Gideon count," and Gideon did, all the way to two hundred and eighty-eight.

Peter pounded his fist on the table. "Two gross!" he yelled.

Adam pounded the table. "Two gross!" he yelled, just like his father.

Gideon pounded the table and yelled "two gross!" and smiled the biggest smile since "Mouse!" on the train.

WEDNESDAY, SEPTEMBER 27, 1871

A letter arrived for Gwen today, and she tore it open and hopped around as if the floorboards had turned to hot coals. "Cager! He's coming to visit!"

Cager is Gwen's younger brother. He is seventeen. "He'll be sweet on you," she said.

Pure, unadulterated guilt crossed her face. "I told him all about you," she confessed. "Do you have a sweetheart already, Pringle? Somebody special back home?"

I was scrubbing behind Lucy's ears – honestly, that child could grow potatoes there – and stopped in my tracks. Gwen's question caused a host of feelings to swim to the surface.

Gwen noticed that, and she apologized, "I

shouldn't have asked such a personal question. I'm sorry, Pringle. It's just that, well, I really don't know that much about you, do I?"

Well, no, Gwen doesn't, and so I can't expect her to know the longing that her question raised in me. Was Rabbit my sweetheart? Perhaps once upon a time, another rabbit hole ago.

Watching Peter and Gwen together makes me wonder: It's clear that they come from two different worlds and yet they have forged a happy life together. Was such a life possible for me, with someone like Rabbit?

FRIDAY, SEPTEMBER 29, 1871

A MESSAGE FOR PETER

It was growing dark as I headed to Peter's office and by the time I arrived, the building was silent. All the other offices had emptied for the night. Gideon wanted me to see his favorite kitten.

Peter was chewing on the end of a pencil, staring at a blank sheet of paper so hard I thought his forehead might bleed. I remembered feeling that way when I studied for examinations at Merrywood.

Several books lay open on his desk. Peter glanced up. I gave him a little wave but didn't want to interrupt his thinking, and so I closed the office door and followed the sweeping sound of a broom to the back room.

Gideon made a big show of sweeping the dirt into a dustpan and emptying it in the trash can – he's such a proud worker! – and then opened the closet. The kittens were mewing and tumbling over each other and nuzzling their mother's belly.

Gideon eased a kitten from its mother. My throat caught a little. The kitten was gray striped and the fur on its tiny forehead formed the letter M, just like Mozie. All four paws were as white as cotton. The kitten mewed and clung to my dress with its pointy claws.

"Is he a boy or girl?" asked Gideon.

I turned the kitten over. "Boy," I said.

"Just like Mozie," said Gideon.

At first, I paid no attention to the boots thumping up the stairs. My first thought was Mr.

Wallace, but then my heart quickened as I realized the boots were too heavy and too numerous for one man.

The boots stopped outside the office door. Peter glanced up, and our eyes met. He tipped his head, signaling me to stay back.

"Hide," I said, urging Gideon inside the closet. I followed, taking care not to bump the pails or brooms or the mother cat and her kittens.

I pulled the closet door closed, leaving it cracked open. I grabbed a broom handle and gripped it tightly. If an intruder opened the closet door, the first – and last – thing he'd see was a broom handle aimed for his eye.

A few seconds later, the office door crashed open. Three men rushed toward Peter. One man carried a thick board that he wielded like a club. "That's him," said the largest man. He was ruddy faced with thick dark hair and heavy brow and deep-set eyes and bulldog chin.

The smallest man had sandy hair and a flat, dull face and smashed nose and a right ear that looked like a cauliflower. He reached into his shirt.

A gun! I gasped and nearly cried out. My knees went weak.

But he pulled out a folded newspaper. "We represent certain gentlemen who read your newspaper and don't like what you say," he said, waving the newspaper. "These gentlemen want you to stop causing trouble with your union talk and eight-hour-day talk and talk about equality. These gentlemen asked us to give you that message."

"Who paid you? Whoever they are, they're using you," said Peter. "Can't you see that?"

"I'm going to shut your mouth for you," said the leader, drawing back his fist. "Nobody uses me."

Peter flowed into action so swiftly I could hardly believe what was happening. He ducked and plowed forward with his fists, driving them into the man's stomach. The man grunted and doubled over.

The small man came at Peter, swinging. Peter grabbed his arm and flung him over the desk, letting him crash on the other side.

The third man was on Peter in a rush, wielding

the length of wood like a club. Peter leaned back, and the wood swung in empty air over his head.

Watch out, I wanted to scream. The first man was lumbering toward Peter, carrying a chair. He threw the chair. As Peter ducked, the man with the club smashed the wood against Peter's head.

For a second, Peter stood, dazed. Then he folded to the floor. The larger man caught Peter and pinned Peter's arms behind his back. While he held Peter, the other two men battered him, piling blow after blow into his face and then his stomach.

Finally, the man released Peter. Peter collapsed in a heap on the floor.

"Think he got the message?" said the man who had clubbed Peter.

My heart pounded as they looked around the office. They lit into Peter's things, tossing books and papers to the floor. In one sweep, they tipped the desks and smashed the wooden chairs. They overturned the bookshelves. One of them threw a paperweight through the glass on the door, shattering it.

Gideon whimpered.

"What was that?" said one of the men, looking around.

I let the mother cat squeeze through the closet opening. She scurried into the outer room. "A cat," said the second man, stooping to pet her. "Let it be. I like cats."

Then their boots crunched against the shattered glass and the door slammed behind them.

"We have to help Peter," whispered Gideon, but I shushed him. I waited as they clattered noisily down the stairs, laughing and joking like schoolboys.

I waited until their booming voices no longer echoed up the stairwell.

I waited until their hooting and hollering drifted up through the open window and grew thin in the distance.

Then and only then did I rush to Peter, unconscious beside his desk, praying I wasn't too late.

Tears! They poured down my face as I eased Peter onto his back and saw the blood running down his head and from his nose. I pressed my head to his chest. He was still breathing.

"I need water," I said to Gideon. "Something to wash his cuts."

Gideon rummaged through the bottom drawer of a turned-over filing cabinet and found a bottle of whiskey.

"That'll do," I said to Gideon.

I reached to tear a piece of my petticoat, but Gideon handed me his perfectly folded white handkerchief.

I doused the handkerchief and dabbed the whiskey on Peter's bloodied temple and washed the cut by his left eye. The eye was swollen shut and the skin around it was turning deep purple.

Peter moaned. His good eye fluttered open. He struggled to sit up. "Ouch," he said.

I helped Peter to a sitting position, his back against the desk. "Did I win? What's the other guy look like?"

"You lost," said Gideon.

"Are you certain?"

"I'm certain," said Gideon.

"I was worried about that," said Peter.

Gideon and I helped Peter to his feet. Peter clutched the side of the desk to steady himself. "Look at this mess."

"I'll sweep," said Gideon, jumping up. "That's my job."

"Not now," said Peter. "Tomorrow."

With Peter leaning on Gideon and me, we stumbled our way down the stairs and into the street toward home. It was obvious that every step hurt.

"Peter!" cried Gwen. "What happened? Who did this to you?"

"You should see the other guy," said Peter.

"You lost," Gideon reminded him.

We helped Peter upstairs and into bed. I pulled off his boots and then got the scissors and cut his hair to better see the wound where the board hit him. He has a gash over his right ear and a potato-sized lump.

With her good hand, Gwen soaked a cloth and

wrung it out and washed his wounds until the water ran clear. I bandaged his head with clean, white cloths.

Gwen has pulled a chair close to the bed and won't leave his side. Peter is sleeping now, but I'm worried because one of my classmates had a brother who died from a cracked skull when he fell from his horse.

SATURDAY, SEPTEMBER 30, 1871

Peter slept through the night and into the late morning. At noontime, I brought tea and toast to Gwen, telling her she must eat something.

Blood had seeped through the bandage and onto her good feather pillow, but Peter didn't have a fever, and so I said a prayer of thanks for that, and then I said, "Money can buy another pillow, but money can't buy another Peter."

Gwen wiped her eyes and sniffled. Something passed over her, as if something had dawned on her for the first time. "Pringle, I know you come from a family of means," she said. "I can see it in your hands and in the way you carry yourself and the way you look at things and in the things you assume. I've never asked you outright about your family. What did your father do for a living?"

How could I tell Gwen that Father belonged to the very sort of men that Peter railed against? How could I tell her that Father would have despised Peter's newspaper and the work that Peter did? That he would have called Peter un-American and an anarchist?

I didn't have to. At that very moment, Lucy came flying into the bedroom with a picture she had drawn for her father. While Gwen and I were doctoring, Lucy had gotten into my inkpot. Blue fingerprints dotted her face, her arms, and her dress like huge freckles. "Look at our family," she said.

Her drawing had seven circles with stick arms and legs and four stick fingers and no toes. "That one's you, Pringle," she said, pointing to a skinny oval.

"It's perfect," I said, choking back a sob. I kissed her dear, sweet face and each blue freckle.

LATER

A massive fire broke out at the Burlington Warehouse on 16th Street and the corner of State. Flames blasted out of the roof and heavy smoke blanketed the South Side. Every fireman in Chicago was called to the scene.

Gideon and Adam begged to see the fire. I said, "Fine, let's go," but they said fires were for boys, not girls, and refused to walk with me.

The street was filled with thousands of gawkers. The fire marshal rushed from engine to engine, sweat pouring down his face, urging his men to soldier on.

Someone pointed to a third-floor window. The crowd yelled, "Jump! Jump!" There, a man stood, half in, half out.

Oh, my heart! I never witnessed anything more tragic. Should a person pray that such a man jump to probable death or not jump and face certain death? Why do we glue our eyes to such tragedy? Are we hoping such a man will jump or not jump?

A cry went up from the crowd as the man fell backward into the smoke. I prayed for a merciful end so that he wouldn't suffer.

The building seemed to swell, and then with a roar, its north wall collapsed, sending a tremor beneath my feet. A cloud of dust and smoke mushroomed upward and rolled over all of us.

SUNDAY, OCTOBER 1, 1871

The firemen are still hosing down the ashes from yesterday's fire. It was the city's worst fire in years. The huge warehouse was constructed entirely out of pine, with only a brick façade, and it was stocked full of everything flammable from syrups to whiskeys, all in wooden barrels. It's estimated the fire caused over $600,000 worth of damage. The firemen also found the remains of the man who had stood at the window. So sad.

MONDAY, OCTOBER 2, 1871

Two nights in a row I have been troubled by a nightmare. It's the same dream. A great monster is chasing me, and I am running down dark streets and alleys, looking for a way out. I thrash myself awake and lie there, afraid to shut my eyes.

Peter stayed in bed all day Saturday and Sunday, but when I came home from market, he was sitting in the parlor. He is still pale and his head aches so much that his eyes are bright with pain. I helped Gwen peel away the bandage to wash his wound. It's healing and shows no sign of infection, although it still looks tender.

Gwen lathered Peter's face and shaved him. Now he doesn't scare Sallie and she'll sit in his lap again. She points to his bandage and says, "Ouchy?" and then she toddles over to the sugar bowl and fishes out two lumps, one for her father's ouchy head and one for herself.

TUESDAY, OCTOBER 3, 1871

Last night, I heard Gwen and Peter talking, and even though I knew I shouldn't listen, I rested my ear against the bedroom wall.

Peter tried to downplay the attack. "Those men can't see that they're pawns. They are hired to break the very unions that could help them. The industrialists know what they're doing: If they pit worker against worker, immigrant against immigrant, they'll never have to worry about paying higher wages or an eight-hour day or safer working conditions."

"Pawns or not, those men are criminals," said Gwen. "They attacked you and destroyed your property. You must tell the police."

"And what would the police do?" said Peter. "Those men are long gone. Some might say I had it coming." As soon as he said that, he laughed, and after he laughed, he said, "Ouch."

Gwen said, "Where does it hurt?" and he said, "My stomach. It hurts to laugh."

"Serves you right," said Gwen. "This is no laughing matter."

Peter didn't say anything for a minute. Then he said, "If you want me to shutter up my newspaper and stop my union work, I'll talk to Robert Lincoln tomorrow. I'll ask if his practice has need for another lawyer."

"Right now, I hate your work," said Gwen. "Most of all, I hate that it's so necessary. Someone needs to speak out and fight for the Isaiahs of the world."

Then Gwen said, "Besides, I don't like Robert. You know he thinks his mother's insane. Poor Mrs. Lincoln. She's lost a husband and three sons. She needs to find her way out of her grief. Can't Robert see that? I don't know what I'd do if I lost you or one of our children."

Then Peter said something I didn't hear and Gwen murmured something else and then they both murmured something and I knew she was no longer angry with Peter.

WEDNESDAY, OCTOBER 4, 1871

WHERE GWEN FINDS HOPE

Gwen wanted Peter to stay home and recuperate one more day, but he said no, that he had an editorial to write and a newspaper to publish. "I need to get to the office before Mr. Wallace so that I can find the key to the toilet." He winked at Gideon, who said, "I'm not telling. Nosiree," and he buttoned his lip.

Gwen didn't want Peter to walk alone, and so I excused Gideon from his morning lessons. After

Peter and Gideon left, I asked Gwen about Isaiah and why Peter had to fight for him. "You heard us talking?" she said, and I grew embarrassed and said, "The walls are very thin."

Gwen stared into her teacup, and I said, "You have a habit of looking for answers in your tea leaves."

"Where there's tea, there's hope," she said. "That's what my mother used to say."

She set the teacup down. "Isaiah was my younger brother. He died in the Avondale mine disaster two years ago."

My heart turned over, hearing that. I wanted to go to her, to throw my arms around her. But I didn't. Something stopped me and kept me at arm's length.

"The law required mines to have a second entrance," said Gwen. "But the law didn't apply to the mines in Luzerne County. Do you know why?"

I saw a flash of something familiar in her eyes. I didn't know what it was. I tried to put my finger on it but couldn't.

"Because a state senator blocked the law. He

was protecting his wealthy friends, the colliery owners," said Gwen. "He was saving his friends the expense and trouble of a second entrance. A second entrance reduced their profit."

She went on to say that Isaiah didn't want to work in the mines the rest of his life, that he wanted to go to school, that he wanted to be somebody, and that Isaiah's death was hardest on Cager, because they were twins.

In the parlor, Sallie began to cry. "Even a rabbit hole has two entrances," said Gwen as she pushed away from the table. She went to the baby.

I wanted to tell Gwen that Father was kind and gentle and a man of high principles. But all I could think was this: Father and his friends had used their power and influence to block the mine safety law in Luzerne County.

THURSDAY, OCTOBER 5, 1871

When I wasn't looking, Lucy made herself a butter-and-jam sandwich and got sticky strawberry jam all over the table and chairs, and each time I think I've wiped up all the sticky spots, I find another. Lucy is an ornery and impossibly headstrong child.

FRIDAY, OCTOBER 6, 1871

For days now, the sky has been as bright as brass with no sign of rain. The city is bone dry. My eyes are gritty. With each breath, I'm gulping dust. Not an hour passes that I don't hear the tolling of the courthouse bell and the clanging of a fire truck, and it's all I can do to keep Adam and Gideon from chasing the trucks.

SATURDAY, OCTOBER 7, 1871

A hot wind has been blowing steadily all day, and more stifling heat is predicted. The weather and last week's warehouse fire and Cager take up all the conversation. It's Cager this, and Cager that. The way Gwen talks about her brother, you'd think Prince Albert was coming to visit.

I sweep the floor and wipe off the furniture and turn around to find another layer of fine dust thick enough to write my name in. It is too hot to cook, but I spent the better part of today making a steak-and-potato pie.

This is how Mrs. Goodfellow says to make pastry for a meat pie:

Sift one pound of flour into a pan. Cut into it three quarters of a pound of beef suet until the flour and suet are crumbly.

Once the suet has *been* worked in, add salt to taste. Moisten the mixture with cold water. Then flour the pasteboard and roll out the pastry, adding thick slices of suet and a dusting of flour between each rolling.

If you can read, you can cook. That's what Gwen says.

Well, I can parse a sentence, recite Latin declensions like nobody's business, discuss paintings and sculpture and Kant's essay on "The Beautiful and the Sublime," and converse in German and French, but I cannot roll out a decent pastry.

But knowing these things does not mean you can cook. I made such a mess I wanted to cry!

After all that work, half the dough stuck to the pasteboard and the other half stuck to the rolling pin. It turned me into a hot, sticky mess, with flour on my face and clothes and my hair and on the floor.

The pastry looked like three layers of wood shingles on a shanty. But Gwen said I did an admirable job. We filled two pies with layers of thinly sliced potatoes and onions and diced steak, and a third with tart baking apples, brown sugar, lemon juice, cinnamon, and nutmeg.

That got me to thinking. I rolled out the scraps of pastry, sprinkled them with cinnamon and sugar, and dotted them with butter, just as Mrs. Robson used to do. I rolled them and shaped them into crescents and baked them.

As the pies baked, Lucy and Sallie played nicely on the floor. Somewhere in the distance, bells pealed and fire pumpers raced toward yet another fire.

Just as I pulled the last steak-and-potato pie from the oven, Peter and Gideon walked in. "I heard the fire trucks and worried Pringle was baking and set the house on fire," said Peter.

Gwen protested. "Peter! That's not nice."

I shook the rolling pin at him, and he held up his hands in mock surrender. "I apologize."

I fetched the cinnamon rolls. Lucy pitched a temper tantrum because she didn't want a roll, she wanted a square, which made no sense at all. It didn't matter. When Lucy is overtired or overexcited, she gets a notion in her head and there's no talking her out of it. She pushed her chair away from the table, slid to the floor, and wailed and rolled around.

"I bet two gross," said Gideon, because 288 is his new favorite number.

Gwen said, "Twenty-five seconds," because she's in a good mood and thinking on the bright side.

Adam said, "Fifty-eight."

Peter said, "Seventy-two. She hasn't kicked the floor yet."

Just then, Lucy kicked the floor. The tantrum lasted eighty-eight seconds.

I pulled Lucy into my lap. We all sat around the table eating the cinnamon rolls, and Peter said, "*Mmm*, delicious." I felt as full of happiness as a person can feel.

LATER

It's well past ten o'clock and impossible to sleep in this heat and so I've taken this diary to the parlor.

A mill has caught fire and the blaze has spread to a nearby lumberyard. The fire is across the river, so there is no need for alarm, but I can see the eerie red glow and hear the tolling of the courthouse bell and the clatter and clanging of the steam pumpers and hose carts. The poor exhausted firemen! How can they battle blaze after blaze?

Outside, a steady stream of people who have nothing better to do for entertainment are passing along our street, heading across the river to watch the fire, shouting and talking and singing as they go. Someone shouted that this blaze promises to be larger than the warehouse fire last week, and I think he sounded too hopeful. Shame on him.

SUNDAY, OCTOBER 8, 1871

A terrible, pungent, smoky smell hangs heavily in the air. The sky is hazy and as stuffy and warm as ever.

This morning, I had a terrible time trying to catch Lucy and hold her still so that I could scrub her face and dress her and tie her hair out of her eyes so that she wouldn't look like a ragamuffin on the Sabbath. Perhaps I wouldn't be so cranky if I wasn't so tired. Perhaps I wouldn't be so cranky if there wasn't so much work to do. But Cager arrives tomorrow and Gwen wants everything perfect.

Ash everywhere! I handed Gideon a broom and told him to sweep the sidewalk and porch. He said, "Not my job," but I said, "Sweep, mister," and he knew I meant it.

LATER

Gideon and Adam begged and begged, and so after our midday meal we walked across the river to see the fire. The air was hot and dry and smelled of smoke. Thin columns of blue smoke were still rising from the piles of coal along the river where, thank goodness, the fire was stopped.

Adam asked if a fire could leap across the river, but Peter said, no, that the river is a natural firebreak.

The sheer scale of the disaster awes me. Four full blocks! Twenty acres of buildings, all burned! All that's left are brick façades that lean at odd angles. Thick ash covers everything like dirty snow. The sidewalk planks are cracked from the heat.

People were picking their way through charred piles of debris, trying to salvage what they could. Firemen were still hosing down pockets of flame. The firemen look exhausted. Their clothing is burned, their skin black with soot and grime, their eyebrows singed, and their eyes bloodshot and swollen from the heat. They fought this blaze for more than seventeen hours. It's Chicago's biggest fire ever.

Peter said we need more firemen, but that the

city won't hire more. Hearing that the city needs more firemen lit up Gideon's face. No doubt he'll be the first to apply.

We returned home, and I told Gideon and Adam there was work to do and I needed help. Gideon called tidying the house "girl's work." Before I turned around, both boys had absconded. I stood on the porch and called and called, but they were long gone.

I was angry, but when I went inside, I spotted Lucy's drawing of her family. I picked it up and looked at the seven blue circles with round hearts and stick arms and legs and my anger melted away. My heart felt full as I realized how far Gideon has come in just a month's time. Not a day goes by that I don't miss my mother and father, but I think they would be happy for Gideon and me. Some families we are given and some families we choose and create for ourselves.

ABOARD THE ILLINOIS CENTRAL TRAIN

1871

MONDAY, OCTOBER 16, 1871

If I ever have a daughter, I will tell her this: Life is full of contraries, and we cannot know happiness unless we have known unhappiness; we cannot know pleasure unless we have known pain; and we cannot know trust unless we have also known betrayal.

Last Sunday, we were walking home from evening church services. Peter was carrying Lucy, who had fallen asleep in the pew. I was carrying Sallie and walking beside Gwen.

I remember how dark the sky was and how brightly the stars shone, and how I still had the tune from the last hymn in my head.

I was thinking, too, about something the minister had said, how he quoted a popular orator named George Francis Train who had spoken the night before. "This is the last public address that will be delivered within these walls!" said Mr. Train. "A terrible calamity is impending over the city of Chicago! More I cannot say, more I cannot utter."

Murmurs of fear rippled through the

congregation. I don't remember feeling afraid. I remember wondering, what sort of calamity? And if Mr. Train knows, why wouldn't he say? Any student of history or the Bible knows that calamity has always been with us, and will always be with us. If you predict a calamity, sooner or later, you'll be right.

As we walked along, these thoughts filled my head. A hot wind gusted down the street, whipping my skirt. It blew Peter's hat off, and Gideon scurried after it. The trees swayed and creaked. Crisp brown leaves skittered across the street.

The courthouse bell tolled. I counted the strokes and then looked across the river. In the west, the sky glowed orange.

"Another fire," said Gwen. "That makes twenty this week. Should we worry?"

"No," said Peter. "We've got the river between us."

The boys ran ahead. Gwen called after them, "Don't go too far!"

But of course they disappeared in the darkness.

We turned the corner onto Sherman Street.

I squinted through the darkness. A lone figure was standing on the Pritchards' porch.

"Cager?" said Gwen, and then "Cager!" She began to run.

Lucy snapped awake and squirmed out of her father's arms. "He's here!" she squealed, and ran to the porch and launched herself headlong into her uncle.

Cager hoisted Lucy in the air. As his duster coattails sailed around him, something began to tick like a clock in my head. He plunked Lucy down.

"You're early," said Gwen. And then, remembering me, she said, "I'd like you to meet—"

Do you know how fast a hummingbird beats its wings? That's how fast my heart fluttered. I don't know why I didn't see the resemblance before—the dark, dark hair, the nose, the chin.

Gwen's brother was Rabbit.

Cager took off his hat. There was something different about his eyes, but the same teasing grin spread across his face. "There's no need for an introduction. Pringle and I are old friends."

The look of astonishment on Gwen's face! "What? What? You know each other?" she said, and then, "Sit, sit" – pulling Cager inside – "I'll pour tea and cut you some steak-and-potato pie – Pringle made it! – and then I want to hear everything."

Inside, we sipped tea and ate pie, and Cager said it was the best pie he'd ever eaten. There was something else, too, something in the way Cager's words trailed off and the way he kept looking around the room as if he expected someone to burst in.

A gust of wind billowed the curtains. The air smelled smoky. The courthouse bell tolled again, indicating the fire had spread to a general alarm.

Outside, people were still making their way down the street. At the sound of the second bell, their voices grew raised and excited as they headed toward the bridge to watch the fire.

The front door burst open, and Adam ran inside, shouting, "It's a big fire! Across the river!"

Adam stopped, nearly falling over his feet. "Uncle Cager!" he yelled, and barreled himself headlong into his uncle, just as Lucy had.

Cager's gaze turned to Gideon, who was standing in the doorway. The color had drained from Gideon's face as if he'd seen a ghost.

"Look!" said Adam. "Gideon peed his pants."

A large wet stain was spreading across Gideon's trousers.

"Gideon," I said. "What's wrong?"

Gideon's mouth was clamped shut, his lips pressed in a thin line. Terror filled his eyes. Then he dashed across the porch and bolted down the street.

If I knew then what I know now, I would have chased after Gideon. I would have followed him. But there's no going back in time, no matter how hard we wish it. We cannot undo the past any more than we can unknow something once we know it.

I tried to sort out what had frightened Gideon, why he peed his pants, just as he had the day he spotted the broken carriage in the carriage house.

The answer hit me, as hard as a rock. "Gideon's afraid of you," I said to Cager.

"Afraid?" said Gwen. "Why would Gideon be afraid of Cager?"

How could Cager not say anything? How could he let me stand there? Did he think I wouldn't fit the pieces together? Did he think I wouldn't turn each piece to see where it fit?

I did, and when the last piece fell into place, it formed a puzzle so terrifying that my hands shook. "What do you know about my parents' accident?"

The look on Cager's face was one I'd never seen before. It was dark and haunted and it turned my backbone to ice.

"Answer me!" I said.

Peter must have arrived at the same equation. "Answer her," he demanded.

Cager washed his hands over his face and swept back his hair. "No one was supposed to get hurt."

Something slithered in the pit of my stomach and crawled up my throat. A scream. I forced it down. "What do you mean, 'No one was supposed to get hurt'?"

"Cager," said Gwen. "What happened?" As she spoke, she moved closer to her brother and put her arm on his. It was then that I knew where her loyalty lay.

Cager's voice sounded hollow and far away. "A few fellas and I wanted to send Mr. Rose a message about the strike. To tell your father what we thought about men like him. We wanted to scare him, to let him know we were serious about our demands."

"Your father," said Gwen. "Your father is Franklin Rose?"

"Yes," I said. "And he doesn't frighten."

"The other fellas and I waited for him. We jumped out. I grabbed the horse's bridle, told Mr. Rose to stop, that we wanted a few words with him. But he wouldn't give us the time of day. To him, we were nothing. He cracked his whip – look, it cut me here" – Cager pointed to the scar on his face – "and said he'd never give in to criminals like us."

He told how the horse reared and bolted, how the buggy jounced, how it tipped as it rounded a bend. How it snapped loose. How Mother shoved

Gideon out, just as the buggy fell over the ravine. How he told Gideon not to say one word.

A hundred pictures flashed through my mind – Gideon, too terrified to talk; my parents' broken bodies at the bottom of the ravine, dead. How could Cager leave flowers and notes at my parents' graves? How could he kiss me and threaten Gideon?

I flew at Cager, screaming, "Murderer!" My hands didn't feel part of me. They felt like somebody else's hands that flailed and scratched and clawed and beat at him.

"Peter!" Gwen cried. "Do something. Stop her!"

Peter started toward me. With both hands, I pushed him away and stumbled upstairs. I shoved Gideon's and my belongings into our carpetbags and headed back downstairs.

Gwen and Cager sat on the divan. His head was buried in his hands, and she had one hand on his shoulder.

"I hope you hang." I spat the words at Cager and left, letting the door bang shut behind me.

Peter called after me, but Gwen said, "Let her

go, Peter. Let her go. I don't ever want to see the likes of Priscilla Duncan Rose again."

ANOTHER MONSTER

In the west, a bright, ruddy light shimmered over rooftops across the river. The night hummed with activity. Carriages clattered up and down the streets. Children played in the street. Men and women hurried past, talking excitedly about the fire as they streamed toward the bridge.

I stood in the middle of the street, doubled over, clutching my stomach and retching and gasping for air. A strong hot wind blew a swirl of brown, withered leaves across the dark street. It tore through my hair and gusted against my face. It stank of smoke, and I remembered I had to find Gideon. For a moment, I considered which direction he might have fled.

In the distance, plumes of smoke rose, dark against dark in the sky. The peal of fire bells floated across the river.

I followed the sound of those bells.

As I crossed the bridge, clouds of smoke buffeted me, stinging my eyes. I soon found myself on De Koven Street, just blocks from the previous night's fire.

Before my eyes, flames shot through shanty rooftops. Pumpers and engines were lined up like cannon. Firemen aimed their hoses and shot streams of water, but the fire was a monster. Its hot breath evaporated the water before it could do any good.

"Stand it as long as you can," shouted a fireman.

Dozens of volunteers formed a bucket brigade that snaked across the street. Each man moved like clockwork, passing bucket after bucket of water. Each bucketful of water drenched one pocket of flame, only for another to spring up elsewhere. It feasted on the wooden sidewalks and streets.

"Blimey!" shouted a man. He dropped his bucket and dashed across the alley. The fire had gobbled up a pine fence and was eating away at a front porch. The man disappeared inside the house.

The fire swirled into the sky, groaning and

howling. A curtain of sparks flew over my head. Debris came down in a shower. I slapped at the stinging embers that landed on my dress.

Men stood on rooftops, smothering small fires with blankets, trying desperately to keep the embers at bay. To my left, a man jumped off his roof just as the roof burst into flames. A burning shingle tore away. The wind carried it upward like a bright kite, then hurtled it several houses away.

An engine came flying down the street. Another fist of flame reared up behind the trees. More flames climbed up a tree trunk. The branches ignited and then fell. Burning leaves swirled about.

A burning tree toppled over, slamming into another house. Flames shot up. The bucket brigade fell apart as the men ran to safety.

The terrible sounds of animals! Mooing, hooves kicking, whinnying, squealing, thrashing as the fire tore into barns and stables.

I called and called for Gideon. I searched around each engine and pumper, asking person after person if they had seen a ten-year-old boy with dark hair. But there were too many boys running around, watching the fire. No one had seen a boy like Gideon.

I didn't know what to do. The gawkers numbered in the hundreds now. Men, women, and children stood elbow-to-elbow, their glowing faces to the sky, watching the fire leap from rooftop to rooftop.

"Not to worry!" someone shouted over the din. "The fire'll burn itself out as soon as it reaches a broad street."

But the fire wouldn't stop at a broad street. It chased itself up and down the narrow alleys and leaped across streets, howling and bellowing as it ran.

The wind increased and began hurling great firebrands across the river. Before my very eyes, a blazing brand sailed like a bright bird across the river, carried by the wind. It lighted somewhere, I didn't know where. Next I heard a whoosh, and rooftops burst into flame.

The fire had jumped the river!

I found myself pulled along with the screaming crowd as they stampeded toward the bridge across the river.

As I headed across the bridge, the wind pushed at my back. I clung tightly to our carpetbags, for fear a looter might wrench them from me.

The bridge was thronged with people, all desperately trying to cross the river, to run ahead of the flames. There were women, their arms piled with bundles. Children clinging to the hems of their mothers' dresses. Hacks lashing their horses, ignoring the pleas for help from those on foot. Horses pulling drays loaded with furniture and bedding and household goods – bed quilts, cane-bottomed chairs, iron kettles.

Once on the other side of the river, I looked back. The west side of Chicago had become a torrent of flames, a fiery sea. I felt crazy with despair. Dear God, I prayed. Where could Gideon be?

My eyes teared from the smoke and ashes and grit. I needed to stop running. I needed to catch my breath. I needed to press my hands to my head and think.

And so I did. I wiped the sweat from my brow on the hem of my dress. My dress had singed holes where embers had fallen and burned the cloth. *Think,* I told myself. *Where would Gideon have gone?*

The answer came to me in a flash, so simple, I laughed. Why hadn't I thought of it before? It was the only other safe place Gideon knew. My mind flashed to the closet at Peter's office, the closet that held the mother cat and the tiger kitten with four white paws that Gideon loved.

I headed toward Peter's office.

I didn't know the time. I only knew the whole night sky was alight. I pressed through the crowd, swimming against a surging tide of people.

I reached the corner of Adams and Franklin. Bits of burning matter whirled and danced over-head. Glowing embers fell like a fiery snowstorm on one rooftop and then another. Within a few seconds, the roofs burst into flame.

"It's headed toward the gasworks," someone shouted.

A new terror seized me.

The heat was scorching, the streets as bright as noon and thick with smoke. Sweat poured down my face and back. But I pushed through the smoke, the orange night sky lighting my way. The howling wind swallowed the tolling of the courthouse bell.

More sparks and cinders burned my skin and singed my dress. My eyes felt swollen from the heat, but at last I reached Peter's office building. I looked up. From a third-floor window, something white – a face – appeared.

"Gideon!" I screamed. "Gideon!"

The face disappeared. Had he seen me? Was he headed downstairs?

I yanked open the door. A gush of heat and smoke pushed me back. I screamed for Gideon. The wind devoured my shouts.

Something brushed past my legs. The mother cat, a black-and-white kitten dangling from her mouth. She scurried across the street.

I pulled my skirt over my mouth and started into the building. "Gideon!" I screamed.

Suddenly, I felt myself pulled from the doorway and dragged across the street. I fought and kicked. "Let me go! My brother's in there!"

Flames burst through the roof. The windows shattered, sending shards of glass flying in all directions. The air thickened and swelled. Then the office building groaned and the walls began to crumble. They collapsed with a terrifying roar and a great mushroom cloud of dark and smoke.

Elsewhere, another mighty roar shook the ground. Another even hotter gust of wind swept over me. The fire had reached the South Side Gas Works.

All around, it stormed cinders and fire. On the ground, I curled into a ball. I didn't want to live. I wanted to die. Now I had nobody. I was alone.

"Get up," said a man's voice.

"I can't."

A hand reached for my hand and gripped it. The hand had quiet, assured strength and later I would recall that I smelled spice and bergamot and orange blossoms. "Get up now," the man said, and I obeyed.

I felt as though I were walking in a dream. I reached the courthouse square. It was crowded with people, holding handkerchiefs to their faces, looking at the courthouse dome. It glowed like a huge torch, golden with flames. Still, the bell tolled, even as flames gobbled up its tower.

The cupola swayed. The bell gave out one last peal, and then the tower collapsed, smashing through one floor after another. Nearly six tons of brass bell landed with a thud that shook the earth. A cloud of debris rose up.

Confusion reached a fever pitch. The roar of the fire grew louder as it gained strength. Women and children dressed in nightclothes staggered under loads on their backs. Horses reared and kicked. Dogs howled and ran in circles. Cats darted in and around legs. Wagons rushed through the streets, laden with dry goods, books, and valuable papers. Men dragged trunks frantically along the sidewalks, knocking down women and children.

The flames seemed to pour down one street

after another like molten lava. We were a river of moving legs and arms, trying desperately to keep ahead of the fire, sweeping eastward, never stopping, until we reached the shore of Lake Michigan.

There, along the shore, we huddled together. I tried to block out the weeping, the moaning, the cries of children searching for parents and mothers calling for their children. I wouldn't look at the blank faces, black with grime; the bleary, staring eyes; the singed hair and clothing.

I felt as though I were sinking, getting smaller and smaller and smaller, as I folded into myself. Too numb to feel anything, I could only watch helplessly as flames and plumes of smoke continued to rise from the city, shuddering with each new explosion.

Daylight came, and the fire continued to gobble up everything in its path, eating its way north, even as the smoke swirled and carried bits of burned material that fell on us like black rain.

Was I hungry? I don't remember. Did I sleep? I

don't know. All I know is that late Monday night, I realized my face was wet. Had I been crying? I couldn't tell. Then my shoulders felt damp. I shivered and drew my arm across my face. My dress was wet, too.

A woman shouted, "It's raining!" and it was true. It was raining, softly at first, no more than a drizzle, but soon the heavens opened up and a steady, hard rain poured down.

Men and women and children cheered and sobbed and thanked God for His mercy. Perhaps I should have thanked God, too. I didn't feel grateful. I had resigned myself to dying. Now, I had to deal with the cold, hard fact that I was going to live.

The next morning, Tuesday, the sun was a crimson ball over the lake. I couldn't look at it. I wasn't ready for evidence that something greater than the fire was at work.

Late Tuesday morning, word spread that Erie trains carrying donations of food and emergency relief had arrived – and more were on the way. My first thought? If a train can enter the city, it can also leave the city. I wanted out of Chicago as quickly as possible. There was nothing here for me anymore.

I left the lakeshore and wound my way through the burned streets. Without the courthouse, I had nothing to direct me. Every street looked alike with its smoking black heaps that had once been houses and stores and churches. The trees were bare and blistered. Their black branches pointed northeast, the direction of the fire.

Smoke filled the air, making it hard to breathe. I told myself that I was headed for the Illinois Central Railroad, but found myself seeking out Gwen and Peter's house. I turned onto Sherman Street. Everything was gone. The Pritchard house was nothing but a blackened pile of ash.

What did I expect? To wake up along a riverbank, as Alice did? To find that the fire and the loss of my brother were nothing but a dream?

I sat down where the porch had once been and closed my eyes. I never felt more alone and despondent in my life. No wonder Gideon went away in his head after the carriage accident. I wished I could go away, too, and stay there and never come back. If I knew how to make myself go away in my head, I would have. I truly would have.

I stood, dusted off my skirt, and started toward the train station. I passed men and women and children, moving dreamlike, picking through the rubble.

Two streets over, a small, lone figure sat beside a smoking pile of rubble, making marks in the dirt with a stick. I blinked and rubbed my eyes. It was a figure I recognized with my heart. Gideon!

I shouted his name and ran to him. I threw my arms around him and shed a pool of tears over him.

"What took you so long?" said Gideon.

I had counted the streets wrong. I had been waiting on the wrong street in front of the wrong house all along.

There is no going back in life, just forward. In five days, this train will arrive in San Francisco, where Gideon and I will begin a new life. I have many skills. I can cook. I can clean. I can take care of children. I can teach.

Before we left Chicago, I sent a telegram to Mr. Royce, my father's lawyer.

Gideon and I are alive and well.

Tell Uncle Edward I'll return for our inheritance when I'm 21.

Our old life would end here except for one more thing. No sooner had the train whistle shrilled and the great wheels began to roll, than Gideon's carpetbag swelled and made a tiny sound.

I unsnapped the carpetbag and—oh, my paws and whiskers!—a gray-striped kitten with white paws peered back at me with wide green eyes.

"Gideon, this has to stop," I said.

EPILOGUE

After Pringle and Gideon arrived in San Francisco, Pringle worked as a nursemaid for a wealthy family in the Haight-Ashbury district. She spent her wages on books and continued her studies. At sixteen, Pringle took her teaching examination and was hired to teach eighth grade in a public school. Gideon attended classes and graduated from the sixth grade when he turned seventeen.

In 1878, when Pringle turned twenty-one, she returned to Scranton. Her uncle Edward had passed away the year before, and Aunt Adeline was stunned when Pringle showed up. Adeline was even more stunned when Pringle booted her out of the house. Pringle promptly sold the house to a doctor, the colliery to the railroad, and withdrew her inheritance from the bank. She installed a large monument to mark her parents' graves.

Pringle returned to San Francisco, and with

her inheritance, she opened a private school, Miss Rose's School for Girls. She located Mrs. Goodwin and Mrs. Robson and hired them to work at the school. The school curriculum emphasized the classics but included practical skills such as cooking, sewing, and housekeeping.

Gideon worked as a custodian and groundskeeper at Miss Rose's School for Girls. He never quit his one bad habit of bringing home stray pets. His menagerie included a parrot that he rescued from a tree, four dogs, ten cats, a goat that followed him like a dog, and a pet rabbit that soon turned into twenty-one rabbits and Pringle said, "Gideon, this must stop." At summer break, Gideon gave each pupil a rabbit to take home. In 1880, Gideon caught pneumonia and died in his sleep. He was nineteen.

In 1892, a new girl enrolled in Miss Rose's School for Girls. It was Merricat's daughter. The two favorite friends were reunited and continued their close friendship for the rest of their lives. Pringle never married.

Pringle's cousin, Ellen, never lost her love of

theater. At sixteen, she ran away with the magician in a vaudeville act. Her mother never spoke to Ellen again. Today, Adeline's statue *The Foundling* would have been worth more than $1,000.

Pringle never saw the Pritchards again. She wrote to the Scranton police department, reporting Cager's involvement in her parents' death, but neither Cager nor his accomplices were found. Cager is presumed to have died during the Chicago fire.

Pringle never ate licorice again, but her favorite book remained *Alice's Adventures in Wonderland*. One day, over afternoon tea, Pringle read her diary aloud to Merricat, who was amazed at Pringle's courage. "There ought to be a book written about you, that there ought," Merricat said, which is almost nearly what Alice said.

"That there ought," said Pringle.

Pringle's diary became a bestselling novel, published in 1905. While touring England in April 1906, Pringle was devastated to learn about the terrible earthquake that struck San Francisco and destroyed her school. Fortunately, her school wasn't in session, and so no students' lives were lost. Pringle bought a cottage in England's Lake District and lived out her life there, writing children's books and painting and reading.

LIFE IN AMERICA IN 1871

HISTORICAL NOTE

Pringle Rose, her brother Gideon, their family and friends, and other characters in this book are products of my imagination, but the details of their lives and the anthracite coal miners' strike of 1871 and the Great Chicago Fire are as true as true can be.

DIARY KEEPING

In the nineteenth century, girls from middle- and upper-class families were encouraged to keep diaries. Many girls like Pringle were given a diary as a special birthday present from their mothers, who believed diary keeping would encourage self-discipline, nurture good character, and help their daughters grow into respectable young women.

For some girls, diary keeping was a social activity. At boarding schools, girls wrote expressively in their diaries and in each other's. (Sharing a diary was a sign of a special friendship.) At home, mothers and daughters often read aloud from their diaries. Some mothers wrote helpful notes in the margins and offered suggestions. For other girls, diary-keeping was a private activity that allowed them to take risks and explore their feelings.

BOARDING SCHOOLS

In the United States, girls attended private boarding schools as early as 1742, when a sixteen-year-old countess named Benigna von Zinzendorf founded Moravian Seminary for Girls in Bethlehem, Pennsylvania.

By 1871, the number of private schools for girls was on the rise. Most boarding schools did not think a girl's academic education needed to equal a boy's. These schools emphasized traditional values, preparing girls for their future roles as wives and mothers and in service to others.

But some more progressive schools offered a rich and varied curriculum, including subjects such as Latin, French, German, spelling, reading, arithmetic, trigonometry, history, and geography, as well as chemistry, physiology, botany, geology, astronomy, and daily exercise.

LABOR UNREST IN AMERICA

As the Industrial Revolution transformed America, men, women, and children labored long hours – usually ten to sixteen hours per day, six days a week, for low wages – in mills, factories, mines, and other industries. The workers had no vacation or sick days. They had no paid holidays. They suffered dangerous and unsafe working conditions.

Many workers immigrated to the United States from other countries. Some of these workers came from countries where workers had already begun to organize and were fighting for an eight-hour workday and other concessions from their employers. In England, women and children had won a ten-hour workday.

By 1871, American workers were forming unions in order to fight for higher wages and better working conditions. Workers had learned that when they united, or unionized, and acted as a group, they stood a better chance of making their employers agree to their demands.

In the beginning, employers tried to prevent unions from forming, and even attempted to destroy unions. They refused to "recognize," or to deal with them. If workers went out on strike, the employers hired other workers, known as *strike-breakers* or *scabs*.

Other people opposed unions, too. In the eyes of the public, the employers were important men who invested their money, created jobs, and made the growth of the industry—and therefore the country —possible. The public worried that higher wages would mean higher prices. Furthermore, most employers were native-born Americans, whereas workers tended to be new or recent immigrants. For these reasons, many native-born Americans sided with employers, not the strikers.

In 1868, anthracite coal miners formed the Workmen's Benevolent Association (WBA). In early January 1871, anthracite coal miners went out on strike for the third time in three years over the issue of wage cuts.

After the striking workers rioted in Scranton on April 7, 1871, the Pennsylvania governor sent in the militia. Despite martial law, the riots continued, especially as some men quit the strike and returned to work. A shooting incident killed two striking workers.

On May 22, the striking men agreed to a compromise: They would return to work and their grievances would be decided by arbitration.

During arbitration, an arbiter acts as a judge, listening to both sides and then deciding the verdict. After influential men depicted the striking workers as criminals, the arbiter favored the employers. As a result, the striking men lost their fight. The mine workers were given wage cuts. Employers were forbidden to hire only union men, which undermined the union's power. This judgment made mine workers more determined than ever.

Over the next five years, several more bitter strikes took place as the miners continued their fight for an eight-hour workday, higher wages, better working conditions, and recognition of their union.

WORKERS UNITE

As labor unions continued to grow throughout the United States, employers continued to oppose unions. (By 1900, Chicago became one of the most heavily unionized cities in America—and a center of anti-unionism.)

Employers fired workers who belonged to unions or who were sympathetic to unions. They recruited strikebreakers, or men who crossed the picket line to replace the striking workers. They created or exacerbated tension between ethnic groups in order to divide workers. They vilified unions and depicted unionized workers as criminals, calling them anarchists and Communists.

Employers turned to lawmakers for help in enacting laws against unions. They also hired thugs to attack union leaders and union sympathizers. They formed private, armed militias and created their own police force, such as the Coal and Iron Police in Scranton and the Pinkertons in Chicago.

After many bitter battles, unions won recognition and won many gains for workers, including higher wages, shorter workdays, and safer working conditions.

In 1938, the Fair Labor Standards Act (FLSA) established a national minimum wage and time-and-a-half overtime wages in certain jobs. The FLSA also established child labor laws that restricted the employment of children.

PROPERTY LAWS AND THE STATUS OF WOMEN

In the early part of the nineteenth century, women did not have the right to make a contract, which restricted a woman's right to buy or own property. She could not keep the money she earned. She could not vote, run for office, or serve on a jury.

If a woman inherited property or money, everything she owned became her husband's – and remained her husband's, even if they divorced. Her husband controlled all the property. Children were also considered the father's property.

In 1848, New York passed the Married Women's Property Law. A few weeks later Pennsylvania followed suit, and over the coming years, other states would, too. This law gave women the right to retain the property they brought into marriage. The law also protected women from creditors seizing their property to pay their husband's debts.

Some husbands found a way to get around the law. In some cases, wealthy or propertied women were committed to asylums against their will because their husbands wanted to keep the wife's property. Although some women may have suffered mental illness, others found themselves committed when their husband wanted a divorce, or when the women didn't behave the way society expected a wife, mother, or daughter to act. For example, one woman was committed when she got a job without her husband's permission. Another woman was committed because she held strong opinions that differed from her family's views.

CHILDREN WITH DISABILITIES

Although it's never stated in the story, Gideon

Rose is a child with Down syndrome. His character was inspired by a man named Sal Angello, whom I knew for many years and to whom this book is dedicated.

Although the characteristics of Down syndrome were identified in 1866, it took nearly one hundred years for a French physician to discover that the syndrome was the result of a chromosomal abnormality. His research led him to the fact that people with Down syndrome have 47 chromosomes, whereas people without the syndrome have 46. A few years later, it was discovered that chromosome number 21 contained an extra partial or complete chromosome in people with Down syndrome.

No one knows what causes the presence of an extra chromosome 21. The extra chromosome can come from the mother or the father, but most likely the mother. It is not hereditary. At this time, there is no way to predict whether a parent carries the extra chromosome.

Babies with Down syndrome are born into all kinds of families, regardless of race, religious background, or economic situation. Thanks to modern medicine, increased awareness, and family and community support, people with Down syndrome live full, rich lives as family members and contributors to their communities.

AMERICAN SOCIETY FOR THE PREVENTION OF CRUELTY TO ANIMALS (ASPCA)

The nineteenth century is also marked by a concern for the rights of animals. Henry Bergh founded the American Society for the Prevention of Cruelty to Animals (ASPCA) in New York City in 1866. The ASPCA is the oldest and first animal welfare organization in the United States. By 1888, thirty-seven out of thirty-eight states in the Union had enacted anticruelty laws.

Ironically, the United States enacted laws to protect animals from cruelty before it had laws to protect children. In 1874, when Henry Bergh learned that a nine-year-old orphan girl was routinely beaten and neglected at her foster home, he consulted his attorney. The attorney argued that laws to protect animals should not be greater than laws to protect children and won the right to remove the child from the foster home. Later, Bergh and his attorney created a charitable society devoted to child protection, the New York Society for the Prevention of Cruelty to Children. It was the first such organization in the world.

RAILROAD TRAVEL

The nineteenth century is also marked by great changes in transportation, thanks to development of the railroad and the completion of the transcontinental railroad in 1869. Despite great advances in railway travel, it took a passenger between thirty and forty-some hours over approximately three days to travel from Scranton, Pennsylvania, to Chicago, Illinois, depending upon connections. The route that Pringle takes is based on a railway timetable from the period.

The train wreck that occurs in Pringle's story is a product of my imagination, based loosely on an actual train disaster that occurred outside Angola, New York, on December 18, 1867, when a faulty axle caused two cars from the Lake Shore Express to derail and uncouple as the train approached a bridge. The rear car crashed down the icy embankment and burst into flames. The second-to-last car fell down the opposite embankment, splintering into pieces. Forty-nine passengers died. Most were burned to death. Just before the accident, thirty-nine-year-old Benjamin Franklin Betts felt a trembling motion and quickly moved to a forward car, an action that may have saved his life.

THE GREAT CHICAGO FIRE OF 1871

In October 1871, Chicago was a tinderbox. The downtown had tall wooden buildings, large wooden cornices, long wooden signs, and mansard-style top stories of wood. Chicago had miles of wooden streets and sidewalks.

Middle- and upper-class neighborhoods had wooden-frame houses and wooden roofs covered with felt, tar, and shingles. In the poorer neighborhoods, homes were built close together with small yards. Pine fences separated the dwellings and penned in livestock. With winter approaching, residents piled wood and wood shavings. They heaped hay in sheds and barns to feed livestock. In other areas, kerosene was stored.

Chicago had fires before. The previous year, the city firemen battled 669 fires. But this October was different. The city was dried out from a long drought. The firemen were exhausted from battling nearly daily blazes, and equipment was badly damaged.

On Sunday, October 8, 1871, Mathias Shaefer stood sentry duty on the courthouse tower. As Shaefer looked through his spyglass, he noticed blue curls of smoke rising from the still-smoking coal banks along the Chicago River. The smoke was leftover from the previous night's fire that had razed sixteen blocks on the West Side.

Then Shaefer spotted flames near Canalport Avenue and Halsted Street. He reported the fire to William Brown, the night operator, and told him to strike alarm box 342. Brown pulled the alarm. A few seconds later, the nearly 11,000-pound courthouse bell tolled, warning the city residents. Firemen headed for Halsted Street.

From the balcony, Shaefer continued to watch

the fire. Suddenly, he realized he had made a mistake. The fire wasn't near alarm box 342. It was near 319. Quickly, he told Brown to strike box 319.

Brown refused. It might confuse the fire companies, he said. And besides, the firemen would pass 319 on their way to 342. (Unknown to Shaefer, a storekeeper had already reported the fire, but the alarm failed to register at the courthouse.)

As Brown predicted, the Little Giant fire company had spotted the fire, and a steamer was headed to the scene, a cow barn at 137 De Koven Street. Within forty-five minutes, seven fire companies were fighting the blaze.

But the fire companies arrived too late and conditions were too great. In less than an hour, the fire consumed an entire block of shanties and was heading for the planing mills, furniture factories, and lumberyards near the river. At first, firefighters and onlookers believed the fire would burn itself out, once it reached the razed area or the river.

They were wrong. At 11:30, a flaming mass swirled over the river. It landed on a horse livery stable and struck the South Side Gas Works. Now the fire was headed in two directions, eating its way north and south.

The fire burned for thirty hours, leaving a swath of burned-out buildings four miles long and one mile wide. It seemed like a miracle when it rained Monday night and into Tuesday.

All in all, it's estimated that at least $200 million worth of property was destroyed. (That's over $3 billion today.) The fire consumed seventy-three miles of wooden streets and 17,450 buildings. It left 100,000 homeless and an estimated 300 people dead and another 200 missing. (Only 120 bodies were recovered.) We'll never know the exact number.

One of the great ironies of the Chicago Fire is the fact that another, even greater fire occurred at the same time in the small lumber town of Peshtigo, Wisconsin, where lumbermen cut timber for buildings in Chicago. The fire tore through the streets so quickly that scores of people could not outrun it. The town's population was about 2,000. Over 1,100 people were killed in the fire.

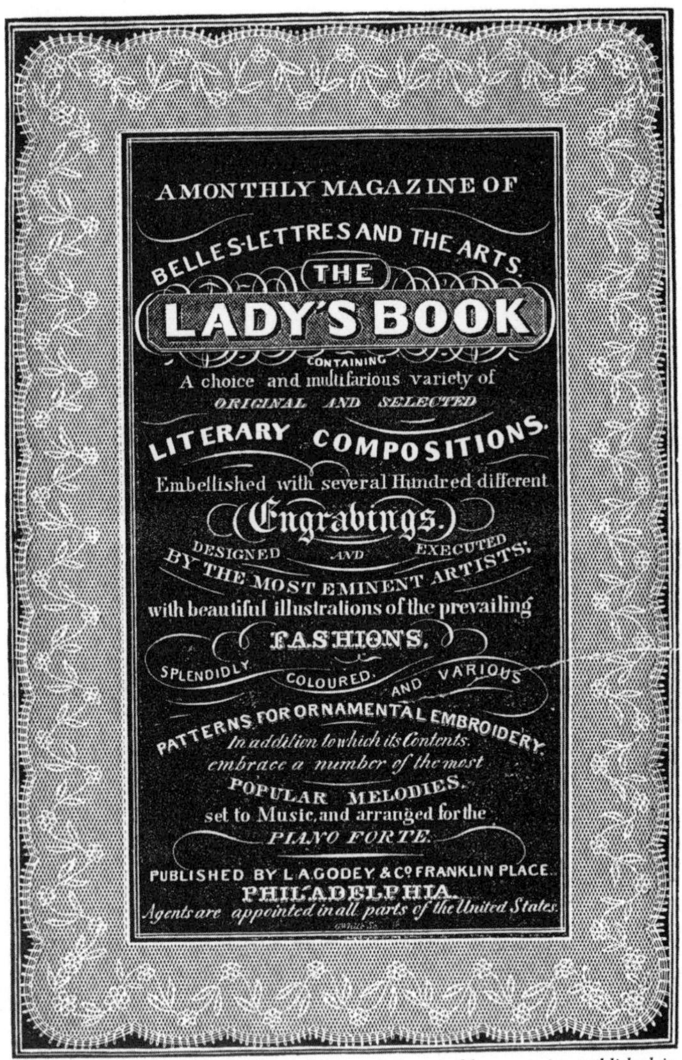

A MONTHLY MAGAZINE OF
BELLES-LETTRES AND THE ARTS.
THE
LADY'S BOOK
CONTAINING
A choice and multifarious variety of
ORIGINAL AND SELECTED
LITERARY COMPOSITIONS.
Embellished with several Hundred different
(Engravings.)
DESIGNED AND EXECUTED
BY THE MOST EMINENT ARTISTS;
with beautiful illustrations of the prevailing
FASHIONS,
SPLENDIDLY COLOURED, AND VARIOUS
PATTERNS FOR ORNAMENTAL EMBROIDERY.
In addition to which its Contents,
embrace a number of the most
POPULAR MELODIES,
set to Music, and arranged for the
PIANO FORTE.
PUBLISHED BY L.A. GODEY & Co. FRANKLIN PLACE.
PHILADELPHIA.
Agents are appointed in all parts of the United States.

Godey's Lady's Book *was a popular women's monthly magazine published in Philadelphia during the mid-nineteenth century.*

Protesting the dangerous and inhumane working conditions to which they were subjected, workers in the coal mines, or collieries, of northern Pennsylvania began to unionize and strike in the mid-1800s. Colliery owners, refusing to succumb to the demands of the workers, often brought in "scab" workers to take the place of the men on strike, thereby maintaining the terrible conditions. In this March 1871 illustration from Leslie's Popular Monthly, *a crowd of miners and their wives are taunting the scab workers. In early April, the strike turned so violent in Scranton, Pennsylvania, that the governor sent in the militia.*

The Avondale Mine Disaster took place in Plymouth, Pennsylvania, on September 6, 1869. When the lining of the mine shaft caught on fire and collapsed, over 108 men and boys were trapped and suffocated, making this tragedy one of the worst mining disasters in Pennsylvania history.

The grim aftermath of the Avondale Mine Disaster.

By the middle of the nineteenth century, Chicago was the primary transportation hub of the continental United States. The city had rapidly expanded, and by 1870, many of the sidewalks, streets, and buildings had been raised for the implementation of the nation's first underground sewage system. However, most of the construction was built entirely of wood. The summer of 1871 in Chicago was extremely dry, leaving the ground parched and the city vulnerable to fire.

The Cook County Courthouse was a remarkably beautiful landmark in Chicago before the Great Fire.

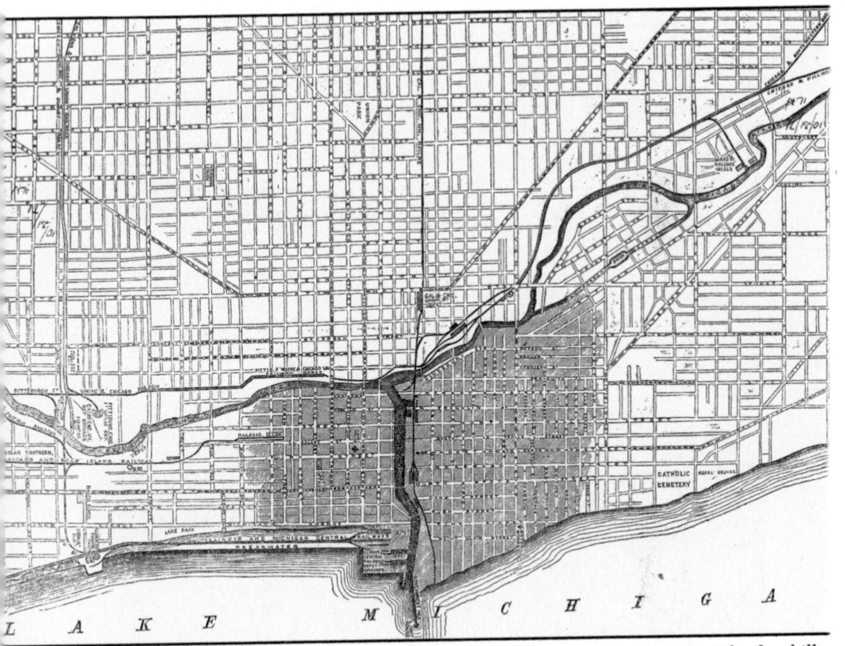

his map illustrates the spread of the Great Fire over three days, October 8–10, 1871. The fire killec timated 300 people and left another 100,000 homeless. At least $200 million worth of property was destro e equivalent of over $3 billion today.

On Sunday evening, October 8, 1871, a raging fire erupted in a barn owned by Patrick and Catherine O'Leary at 137 De Koven Street. The next day, the Chicago Evening Journal *reported a rumor as a fact: that the fire was caused "by a cow kicking over a lamp in a stable in which a woman was milking." To this day, the actual origin of the fire is still unkown.*

Not realizing how quickly the fire would spread, thousands of people turned out to watch the excitement.

Steam-powered fire engines, like the one depicted here, were used during the Great Fire of Chicago.

Two men stand in the ruins of what was once the northwest corner of Washington and LaSalle streets.

The fire destroyed nearly $200 million worth of property, leaving Chicago in ruins. An incomplete set of columns stands in place of what used to be the Fifth National Bank on the northeast corner of Clark and Washington streets.

Chicago's first railroad depot, Union Depot, built in 1848, was destroyed by the Great Fire, leaving the station a wreck.

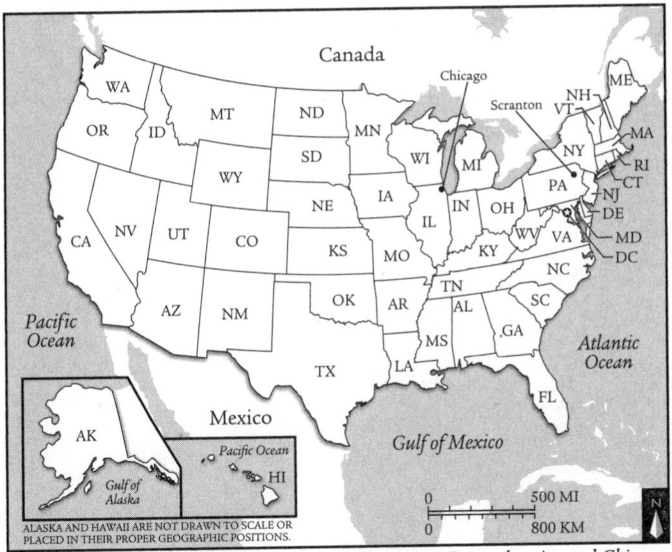

A modern map of the United States showing Scranton, Pennsylvania, and Chicago, Illinois.

The character of Gideon, Pringle Rose's younger brother, was inspired by a family friend named Sal Angello, shown here.

"BEAUTIFUL DREAMER"

(serenade)

Words and Music by Stephen C. Foster 1865

Beautiful dreamer, wake unto me
Starlight and dewdrops are waiting for thee
Sounds of the rude world
Heard in the day
Lull'd by the moonlight have all pass'd away

Beautiful dreamer, queen of my song
List while I will thee with soft melody
Gone are the cares of life's busy throng
Beautiful dreamer, awake unto me!
Beautiful dreamer, awake unto me!

PASTY

Steak and potato pies known as pasties are believed to have originated in Cornwall, England, where they were a staple food of workingmen, especially the mine workers. Records show that children who worked in the mines often carried the individual meat pies as their snack or lunch.

When English and Welsh mine workers immigrated to America, they brought their love for pasties.

Miners relished pasty, not just because of how delicious it is, hot or cold, but also because it's moist. In the dust-filled coal mines, mine workers needed something moist to eat for their midday meal, to help get the coal dust out of their mouths and throats.

I have always admired the way my mother could roll out three or four pie crusts with ease. (The pie-crust rolling gene skipped me.) My mother's pasty is delicious. Here is her recipe:

PIE CRUST FOR 9-INCH PAN:

2 cups flour
1 teaspoon salt
2/3 cup shortening
6 tablespoons water

Measure flour and salt into large bowl. Cut shortening into flour. Sprinkle in water, one tablespoon at a time until flour is moistened and dough comes together.

Divide dough in half. Sprinkle flour over board. With floured rolling pin, roll dough two inches larger than pie plate. (This is where my mother says, "Don't be afraid of the dough.") Fold pastry into quarters and ease into pie plate.

After pie is filled, repeat with remaining half of dough.

STEAK-AND-POTATO FILLING:

1 1/2 pounds sirloin steak, trimmed and cut into 1/2-inch cubes

3 medium potatoes, peeled and sliced thin
1 medium onion, finely chopped
2 tablespoons flour
3 tablespoons butter
salt and pepper to taste

Layer one third of the steak, potatoes, onions, flour, and butter into bottom crust. Repeat two times. Cover with top crust. Trim excess dough. (Save dough scraps for cinnamon and sugar pastry.)

Moisten top crust with cream or milk. Bake at 400 degrees for 50–60 minutes.

CINNAMON AND SUGAR PASTRY

In our house, scraps of pie dough were rolled into cinnamon and sugar pastries. To make your own, simply roll out excess pie crust. Sprinkle cinnamon and sugar over the dough. Dot with butter. Roll into crescent shape. Place in separate pie plate and bake alongside pasty for about 15 minutes.

AUTHOR'S NOTE

Most stories grow from tiny seeds.

The seeds for Pringle's story were planted when I first read about Jabez in 1 Chronicles 4:10. In this short prayer, I recognized the seeds of a good story. I began to ask myself: What if a girl prayed as Jabez prayed, asking God to bless her, to increase her coastline (often interpreted as wealth or responsibility), to guide her, and to keep evil from her? What if she was given everything she asked for, but in an unexpected way?

Those questions helped to launch Pringle's story. From there, I began to think about the other things a story needs, such as setting and characters. The character of Gideon was inspired by a family friend named Sal Angello, who was born with Down syndrome in 1947.

Although more was known about Down syndrome in 1947 than in 1871, some things remained unchanged. When Sal was about six years old, doctors convinced his mother to send him to Pennhurst State School and Hospital to live. In order for Sal to adjust to his new surroundings, school officials wouldn't permit his family to talk, see, or contact him for one month. His mother couldn't wait the month. After one visit, his mother withdrew him from the school. She was determined to keep Sal home at all costs.

In 1956, *Parade* magazine, a national Sunday newspaper supplement, featured Sal in an article called "The Puzzled World of the Retarded Child." Although the journalist called Sal's life "tragic," his sister, Rose Marie Crotti, is quick to point out that the journalist's article reflects a common attitude of the 1950s—a view based in fear and lack of understanding. This view is not accepted, nor fair nor accurate today. But Rose Marie credits the journalist with addressing the issue, since such disabilities were not often written about at that time.

Sal inspired his sister, Rose Marie, to advocate for children with special needs as a teacher, a principal, a school district superintendent, and as a consultant for the Pennsylvania Department of Education.

Sal died in 2010. He was sixty-two years old.

Susan Campbell Bartoletti is the award-winning author of many books for young readers, including the Newbery-Honor book *Hitler Youth: Growing Up in Hitler's Shadow*; the Sibert Medal–winning *Black Potatoes*; *The Boy Who Dared*, which was an ALA Notable and an ALA Book of Distinction, as well as the winner of the Pennsylvania Carolyn Field Award; another title in the Dear America series, *A Coal Miner's Bride*; and many more. Her work has received dozens of awards and honors, including the NCTE Orbis Pictus Award for Nonfiction, the SCBWI Golden Kite Award for Nonfiction, and the Jane Addams Children's Book Award.

Susan worked as an eighth-grade English teacher; she now writes full time and lives with her family in Moscow, Pennsylvania. She teaches in the brief-residency MFA program at Spalding University in Louisville, Kentucky. You can visit her online at www.scbartoletti.com.

ACKNOWLEDGMENTS

Some day-to-day events leading to the Great Chicago Fire are products of my imagination. Others have been reconstructed through research of contemporary newspapers, books, personal accounts, and maps, as well as books and articles published on the subject in recent years.

In addition to the standard works, I'm grateful to the following: Jim Murphy's Newbery-Honor book *The Great Fire* (New York: Scholastic, 1995); Peter Cookson, Jr. and Caroline Hodges Persell's *Preparing for Power: America's Elite Boarding Schools* (New York: Basic Books, HarperCollins, 1985); Jeffrey Geller and Maxine Harris's *Women of the Asylum: Voices Behind the Walls, 1840–1945* (New York: Anchor Books, Doubleday, 1994); Phillip L. Safford and Elizabeth J. Safford's *A History of Childhood and Disability* (New York: Teachers' College, Columbia University, 1996), and John H.

White, Jr.'s *The American Railroad Passenger Call*, Parts 1 and 2 (Baltimore: Johns Hopkins University Press, 1978).

I'm especially grateful to Lewis Carroll and his classic *Alice's Adventures in Wonderland*, first published in 1865. Lewis Carroll is the pseudonym of Charles Lutwidge Dodgson. Fellow devotees of this work will spot the many references. For this work, I relied on a version electronically published by the Project Gutenberg.

I'm grateful to the many generous people who helped inform this story: Rose Marie Leitza Crotti; Sal Angello; historian Patrick McKnight and curator Sarah Smith (Steamtown National Historical Site, Scranton, Pennsylvania); my editor, Lisa Sandell, for her unflagging support and patience; friends Clara Gillow Clark, Joyce McDonald, and Elizabeth Partridge for reading parts of this story and sharing pages; Bambi Lobdell, just because; my mother, Joan Jenkin, for inspiring me to write about a nanny; my grandchildren for inspiring certain (*ahem*) character traits; and my husband,

Joe, who helped me find the right ending on our many walks around the lake.

Grateful acknowledgment is made for permission to use the following:

Cover portrait by Tim O'Brien.

Cover background: Chicago's Court-House Square on fire, North Wind Picture Archives.

Page 233: *Godey's Lady's Book*, The Granger Collection.

Page 234: Mine strikers, Library of Congress.

Page 235 (top): Avondale Mine Disaster, The Granger Collection.

Page 235 (bottom): Crowd waiting outside Avondale Mine, ibid.

Page 236 (top): View of Chicago before the Great Fire, Topfoto/The Image Works.

Page 236 (bottom): Chicago's Cook County Courthouse, Library of Congress.

Page 237: Map showing reach of the Great Fire of Chicago, The Granger Collection.

Page 238 (top): Catherine O'Leary's cow, ibid.

Page 238 (bottom): The Great Fire, Corbis.

Page 239 (top): Steam-powered fire engine, Keystone Archives/HIP/The Image Works.

Page 239 (bottom): Two men standing in ruins, Library of Congress.

Page 240 (top): Incomplete set of columns of Fifth National Bank, ibid.

Page 240 (bottom): Ruins at Union train depot, ibid.

Page 241 (top): Map by Jim McMahon.

Page 241 (bottom): Sal Angello, courtesy of his sister, Rose Marie Crotti.

OTHER BOOKS IN THE DEAR AMERICA SERIES

Available in print and e-book editions.